The Genesis

of Atron

Book Two

by

Barbara Moon

The Genesis of Atron

Copyright 2009 Barbara Moon

All rights reserved

The Genesis of Atron

Table of Contents

Dedication iv

Thanks iv

Characters v

Map of Atron vii

PART ONE—The Split Parchment 1

PART TWO—Many Changes 83

PART THREE—The People of Tolden 146

Dedication

To

my grandchildren, because above all else I hope the story will help you understand the importance of walking in union with Christ.

And

to Henry Hermann, the first non-family member to tell me how much he liked Book One. Henry, your words touched me and inspired me.

Thanks

To

Chris for suggesting the demise of Brasald.

And

to Bob for editing, formatting and coaching, to Amy for her suggestions and to Debbie for the final note.

The Genesis of Atron

Characters

THE ORIGINALS

Jasend, son of Atlan

Nik, Tyra, Lisond, friends of Jasend and children of Rondel

THE UNIDANS

Vandlyn, father of Damond and early leader of Unidans, husband of Amaz

Damond, friend/husband of Marna, father of Kolen

Eliot, brother of Damond, friend/husband of Serad

Kolen, husband of Elezaban, father of Sandlen

Sandlen, mother of Karand (Gran), wife of Jazen,

Karand (Gran), friend of Lornen, wife of Wilden, mother of Handen

Candra, granddaughter of Karand (Gran)

ELDERS or SCOUTS of UNIDAN

Henric, husband of Janed

Conrand, husband of Deblan

Ryese, father of Lornen, weapon designer and scout, friend of Jazen

Aarnon, scout

2009 Barbara Moon

THE TOLDENS

Brasald, father of Oland and early leader of Tolden

Oland, son of Brasald, adversary of Damond

Kaylan, descendant of the Originals, mother of Eric and Stephad, wife of King Krall

Brinid, daughter of Jired & Darrias

Darrias, sister of Kaylan, wife of Jired, mother of Brinid

Tylina, lady-in-waiting to Kaylan, daugher of Cresta

King Krall, descendant of Originals

Map of Atron

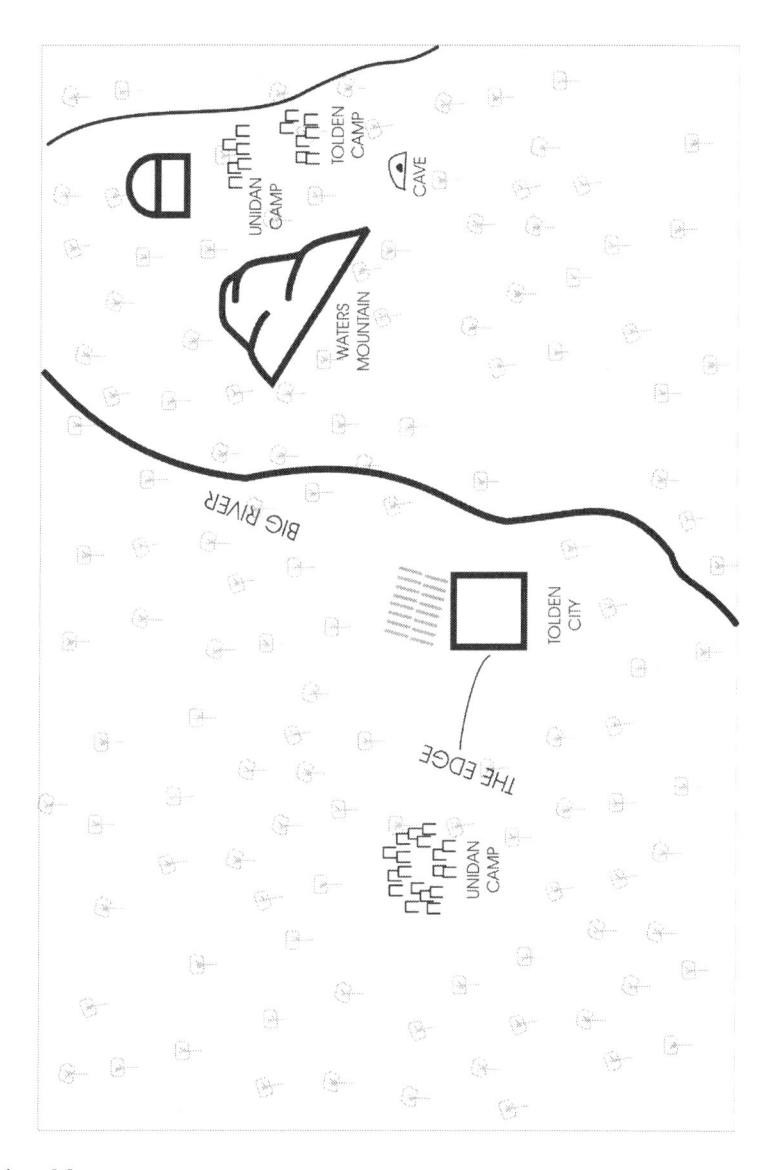

The Genesis of Atron

The Genesis of Atron

PART ONE—The Split Parchment

CHAPTER ONE

EARTHDATE February, 2280

I can't believe it's almost time to leave. Father says we're leaving in two more nights. My heart races just thinking about it. I feel huge knots in my stomach from both fright and anticipation as I sit here in my room writing, most likely for the last time here on Earth. I'm still not certain how I feel about what they're doing. Everything's going to change. Everything. Not one thing will remain of my life as I know it now; nothing I've known for these fifteen seasons. That's the part that scares me. Yes, I'm scared, but I'm trying to see this as an adventure; the beginning instead of the end. What if we get caught? It would mean sure imprisonment for the adults, and I don't want to think about what it might mean for us young ones. I'm glad Nik, Tyra and Lisond are going. At least that won't change. All the parents say it's necessary to leave. They've tried everything. For years they've tried. Yes, I admit I'm scared, but I know that Father and the others know what they're doing. I know we have to go-- it's decided--the preparations are made and we young ones have to trust them. They say each of us has a part and each part is important--that's the anticipation, I guess, waiting to see the good out of it all. I'm going to try to shake off the fear and see the possibilities for adventure before me. And as always, The One is with us. That's what helps me the most. With Him, I can do all things.

Damond closed the Reader he was using, saving his place in Jasend's diary as he leaned back against the tree near his tent. The air was warming and the birds were greeting the dawn. Though Damond had only counted fifteen seasons, he was tall for a Unidan, with dark, shoulder length hair and brown eyes, his face tan from working in the sun. His body was strong from working hard in the fields, carrying water and taking care of the animals. Damond wore dark pants and a dark red shirt, his soft goat skin boots sitting idly beside him, waiting to be laced when the time came to head for the fields. For a few more minutes, he could wiggle his bare feet in the grass before going to gather grain.

Off in the distance he could see the top of the Dome sparkling in the early morning sun. The colors and lights that bounced from its surface were like nothing else on Atron, maybe nowhere else in the galaxy. The Dome housed the MagnaRay which controlled the weather on Atron, making certain there was plenty of rain during the growing season and keeping the seasonal changes mild. Without it there would be no Atron

The Dome. Damond loved looking up from different places he was working or playing and seeing the Dome. He loved it even more when his father took him inside to do research, to read the travel logs or to choose other Readers to go through. Learning why and how Jasend and the other Originals had risked their lives to come here inspired Damond as he read and studied the writings left in the Dome. He knew that without the Originals there would be no Unidans or Toldens on Atron.

Diaries and logs were just two of many different kinds of books left in the Dome by the Originals. Most of the thousands of books brought by the Originals were in Readers, portable machines powered by the sunlight. They were available for pleasure reading or for studying, containing information on many topics. The people could write in the Readers as well, with no need for a writing instrument. Some of the Ancients' books and books of The One were bound in leather with pages made of special paper, and available in both forms, but only the Readers could be taken out of the Dome. Along with the books of The One, the diaries were Damond's favorites. Although he had already begun preparation for his Becoming Day when he completed eighteen seasons, he still loved reliving with Jasend the risks he and the others had endured to make it to Atron.

Becoming Day, a special ceremony begun by the Originals and still celebrated in Damond's time, marked the end of childhood and the entrance into adulthood. A short time before the ceremony, the young people chose a First Companion who would pledge to help them strengthen their skills for living closely with their future Last Companion, with whom they would join for life. The First Companions would speak truth to each other at all times, listen to the other's admonitions and practice openness by staying connected and working through problems. During the ceremony the young people also pledged to keep their bodies pure for their Last Companion. It was a day each Unidan young person looked forward to with great anticipation and when it was over, they were called "Participants."

Damnond's father, Vandlyn, and a man named Brasald, a Tolden, shared the leadership of the people. Through the years, as changes came about on Atron the people had come to refer to their two rulers as kings, but in truth they were simply the chosen leaders. Calling them kings could be misleading, as Unidan and Tolden kings did not live in splendor like the ancient kings that Damond had read about.

The Genesis of Atron

And since one reason the Originals traveled to Atron was because they wanted to begin a new life solely under the rule of The One, Vandlyn discouraged anyone from calling him king. Brasald was not as strict and seemed to enjoy the title. Lately, it had become obvious that there were many things that Brasald and Damond's father did not always see eye to eye on. One of these was the Covenant.

Upon their arrival on Atron, the Originals had made a Covenant that restricted the use of the Dome and its contents. From reading the diaries and logs, Damond knew that his father was strong about following the Covenant from the Originals, but at times it was difficult to know how Brasald and some of his people viewed the pledge to use very little of the technology they had brought with them to Atron.

The Originals had fled Earth's godless society to get away from the machines and technology that had corrupted people's ability to interact and connect with one another. They did not see the technology as evil, but did feel that it was a factor that kept people from truly relating to each other. Most people they knew had turned away from The One and His ways, and the families who had come to Atron believed that hard work and community living would help keep people more in tune with both The One and each other. Their deepest desire was that their children and descendants would know The One and His ways and be able to live peacefully together. Damond knew from reading Jasend's diary that they tried for years to influence the corrupt, self-centered society from which they came, but to no avail. In order to assure their children would have a better life within the ways of The One, they fled.

Although the Originals wished to limit extended use of their technology, the Dome itself was the epitome of technology, technology that enabled colonizing of other planets. But the people of Atron chose to leave the majority of that technology inside the Dome, only entering it now and then to study the ancient books from The One, study their history, maintain the MagnaRay or do various kinds of scientific research. In the camps there were always a handful of people who studied science and medicine using information in the Dome, but they used that knowledge only for life and death issues. The people did not take the marvels inside the Dome lightly or use them haphazardly. They preferred to rely on The One, each other and a simple way of life.

Many items that the people needed for everyday living, such as cooking utensils, tents and tools, were brought on the ship with the Originals to use as they worked to live off the land. The books in the Dome were full of instructions on how to make many useful items that did not require sun power. The Originals also had brought Tazors, a combination sword and energy blaster, and Sedats, a small, versatile knife easily carried and used for cooking or hunting. On Earth Tazors were weapons, but the people of Atron used them for hunting as there was no need for weapons in their society.

After arriving on Atron the Orginals decided that because of their limited resources and their deep desire to build the ways of The One into their children, they would encourage the people to marry after twenty seasons and have small families. The Unidans still followed this concept in order to assure their children plenty of loving attention and quality training.

As Damond sat thinking about the Covenant and how strongly the Originals felt about having a better life for their children, he looked around the camp for his brother, Eliot. His view included the many tents of his people and the activity increasing around the tents as more people stirred to get ready for another day. The camp was surrounded by thick forests filled with good hunting. All through the camp, beautiful flowers grew abundantly, filling the spaces around the tents with colors that contrasted with the dark gray and brown tents. It was almost time for the young people to go to the fields to work before teaching time, and Damond and Eliot usually went together. After their teaching time with the elders they would practice their Tazor drills.

Most days someone in the family gathered grain for making their flat corn or wheat cakes, a staple that was very filling. As the cooler season approached they would gather and grind more grain to store. Gathering grain was not at the top of Damond's favorites, but Tazor drills were. He and Eliot often competed during practice but it was all done in fun, helping them to hone their skills. They were close as brothers are meant to be, working, playing and competing together.

Eliot had not been in their tent when Damond awoke. *He's most likely out with Marna and Serad getting water for Mother*, Damond mused as he stood up and walked towards the tent to put his Reader away. Just as he was coming back out the door he heard his brother calling.

"Damond," Eliot yelled from across the camp. "Come help us with the water. As soon as we eat breakfast, let's get the grain gathered so we can do some extra Tazor practice before teaching time."

Damond smiled and waved at Eliot who was walking towards him with Marna and Serad, their best friends, coming up the slope from the stream, each carrying two hide buckets sloshing with fresh water. "I'd love to get in some extra practice," he greeted his brother.

Eliot, just a bit shorter than his brother had the same dark hair and brown eyes. Both wore the brown work pants and sturdy woven shirts colorfully dyed by their mother from plants that grew around Unidan. In addition to their Tazors sheathed at their sides, they each carried a Sedat in their belts. Marna and Serad, both close in age to the boys, had lighter hair, hanging to their waists, tied at their necks with a strip

The Genesis of Atron

of hide in preparation for a day of work. They, too, wore dark slacks and colorful shirts woven by their mother. Returning Damond's greeting with a smile, their blue eyes lit up as he walked over to meet them and Eliot. Damond hurried to take a bucket from each of the girls, grinning at Eliot as they passed each other. Their mother, Amaz, appeared at the entrance to their tent and took one of the buckets from Eliot as he carried the other inside behind her. Damond went with Marna and Serad to their tent to leave their water there.

Returning to their parents' tent, Damond smelled the delicious odors of cooking meat, eggs and flat corn cakes filling the air as the camp continued coming to life all around them. The young people quickly helped finish preparing breakfast and cleaning up afterwards, and then headed for the fields to gather grain, where working together made for easier work. Teaching time with the elders was usually next, but today they would get in extra of their favorite—Tazor practice.

* * * * * *

"Great shot!" Damond cheered as Marna's Tazor blast hit the target set up several lengths away on a stump. The four had finished their morning work and hurried to the practice stump before teaching time.

Nearby, Eliot and Serad were using their Tazors as swords while Damond and Marna practiced controlling the bursts of energy. Only those who were in tune with The One could manage the energy well without using the buttons on the handle. When the Originals had begun to experiment with the Tazors, they had accidentally discovered that they could make the bursts of light without pushing the red buttons on the handle. It soon became evident that The One was teaching them that He could direct this power, though the Tazor could be used as a sword or with the buttons any time. Since there was no need for defense on Atron, Tazor practice became part of training for

The Genesis of Atron

attuning with The One, for exercise and for self-discipline. The young people loved it.

"Your turn," Marna said to Damond, as she walked back from setting a new target on the stump. "Back up and see how much farther you can make it reach." Marna stepped to the side to watch as Damond took aim.

Damond stilled his heart and breathing, focusing on The One. He knew he could use the buttons on the handle, but he really wanted to control the light from within. The force of the blast was controllable either way when one knew the secret. *Now!* he sensed, and the blast shot forth. There! That was the longest blast he'd ever made and it hit the target, leaving a small blackened hole in the hide.

"An even greater shot!" Marna echoed Damond's words back as Eliot and Serad paused in their practice to look at the distance that Damond was standing from the stump. The smile on his face spread from one ear to the other. He walked over to take a look at the mark on the hide.

"That's about the best I've seen yet," Eliot yelled walking over to Marna. "Would you walk off the steps so I can try that?"

Sheathing her Tazor, Serad laughed at Eliot's anticipation of equaling his brother's skill. "I will carry your water from the stream tonight if you make the same shot," she challenged.

"And if I don't, what will you do?" he queried, turning to look back over his shoulder at the dare.

"If you miss, you'll carry mine for three mornings and three evenings," came back the reply. Serad's blue eyes twinkled with fun.

The Genesis of Atron

"I will not miss," said Eliot confidently as he stepped over to stand on the spot Marna was marking where Damond had been when he took aim. Eliot raised his Tazor, focusing on the hide covering the stump. The light shot out, straight and true, but fell to the ground just short of the stump. The friends broke out in laughter at the picture of Eliot making extra trips to the stream for three days. They always found great enjoyment when there was any reason to have fun with each other.

"Well, The One's books say that pride goes before a fall, so I guess I need to practice a bit more—and focus on The One," laughed Eliot right along with the rest. "I'm glad it's yet warm these days since I'll be sloshing that extra water extra times for a while."

"And what will I do with my newly acquired spare time?" Serad chuckled, eyebrows raised, eyes twinkling. "It will give me more time to use my Reader. I can just sit under a tree and smile every time you go by. What a pleasure it'll be to watch my friend working so hard." Laughing again, she marched right over and hugged the good sport.

"Back to the practice, everyone," Marna chimed in. "Let's all do sword Tazors for a while so Eliot can think of something besides his new chores. It won't be long until it's time to do them. Serad, we shall enjoy watching your well-deserved rest."

"I can't wait for that scene that I see in my mind," Serad answered as she drew her Tazor from its sheath and stood facing Eliot, ready to practice more with her friends.

"It will be a pleasure to sit while you work, my friend. Ready? Begin." The four Tazors clanged as each pair began to practice.

CHAPTER TWO

Amaz and Vandlyn were enjoying the quietness of the evening after a long day. Amaz busied herself making a second cup of tea for both of them. She noticed that her Companion was quieter than usual, his brow furrowed in deep thought.

"Why are you so quiet this evening, Vandlyn?" Amaz asked as she brought the steaming cups to sit beside her husband on the huge pillows beside the small fire inside their tent. "I see that you're thinking of something unusual. What is it?"

Amaz was a beautiful woman, strong and lean with kind hazel eyes. She kept her long, dark hair braided and wrapped around her head during the day while working and caring for her family. Like all young people of Atron, she had been trained in the use of the Tazor as well as daily chores for living. She knew the history of their planet and walked in union with The One. She loved the simple life that the people of Atron lived and was an excellent mother to Damond and Eliot. Amaz waited for Vandlyn to speak.

"I am very concerned, My Love, that something is going on that should not be," he nodded his thanks for the cup of tea, making room for her to sit. "For some time now I have sensed a big change in Brasald and others in his camp. He is not the friend I knew growing up. I feel that way with other Toldens as well--and I've noticed troubling changes in their children."

Amaz sat quietly where she could observe her Last Companion's face while he thought through what he wanted to say. He was a very wise and kind leader, descended from the Original's family that became the Unidans. His brown eyes shone with intelligence and confidence. Vandlyn's brown hair was sprinkled with gray, pulled back with a strip of hide, and barely touching his shoulders when loose. His body was still muscular and lean, tanned from his work in the fields. He loved to read and talk of the Ancients and the Originals. He held strongly to the Covenant they had made after leaving Earth to work hard and be interdependent on each other, agreeing to use as little of the marvels in the Dome as possible. Most of all he walked closely with The One Within and knew Him well.

Amaz was disturbed by Vandlen's comments. "That sounds very serious," she said as she mirrored her husband's face and sipped her tea.

"I'm not yet sure, but I've been watching," said Vandlyn thoughtfully. "And there's something at the Dome. Something is going on there that I cannot put my finger on."

Amaz nodded and warmed her hands around her tea, waiting for Vandlyn to continue. He was not one to worry or one to overreact. If he was concerned, something was there.

"I've noticed that more activity has been going on around the Dome, people in and out more than usual. Brasald is one of them. That concerns me the most."

Though all Originals followed The One and all Originals made the Covenant about the Dome, Vandlyn sometimes wondered if Brasald was really following The One or the Covenant as he claimed. But to question his old friend would be very serious; he would have to have evidence.

"What will you do?" Amaz asked quietly.

"I'll keep watching. I might confront him if I feel more strongly that something isn't right. And I'll continue to listen to The One and talk with Him. He will direct me."

The Genesis of Atron

Amaz balanced her cup as she nestled into Vandlyn's arm upon the pillow and rested her face on his chest. There was not much to do except wait, watch and wonder. The One had always been clear and would direct now. And Vandlyn would know.

CHAPTER THREE

Brasald stole swiftly through the Dome's door, sliding it closed as the lights came on. He was a small man with short curly hair and dark beady eyes, his mouth turned down in a frown. It was extremely important that his late night visits in the Dome go undetected. Hardly ever did anyone go to the Dome at night and then not alone.

He quickly shut down the main lights and walked towards the laboratories. Vandlyn would not be happy if he knew of any unauthorized visits. *I have my reasons*, Brasald thought as he moved carefully inside the dark building. *The formula and those plants I've been experimenting with may hold the key to faster growth that will increase my crops, make less work and pave the way for us to break away from Vandlyn and his families. I'm more than ready to lead on my own. It's time to break the Originals' Covenant and use the resources here in the Dome. Years have passed and we still live simply and in their old ways. Some of us Toldens are sick of it with all that's here for the using. When I finish what I'm doing here, even Vandlyn will agree—and if he doesn't, then we will go on without him. There's plenty of room for us to spread out as we please.*

Reaching the lab and turning on the lights, Brasald took some large vials from under one of the cabinets. He held them up to the light and looked at the orange liquid inside them. It was almost perfected. Only a few more nights and he would be ready to spray some of it on a section of the plants outside. Then he would be able to determine what the end result would really be. Working diligently there in the lab gave Brasald time to plan his next move after that.

What was that? The sound of the door opening startled Brasald out of his musings. *Who else would be coming in at this time,* he thought as he moved the vials back under the cabinet. It was too late to hide or turn off his light. "Who's there?" he demanded.

"It is I, Father," he heard his son, Oland, call out. Oland was a burly young man, heavily built with black hair hanging over very dark eyes. His brow was habitually in a frown and the stubble on his cheeks made him look older than his seventeen seasons.

"What are you doing here?" Brasald growled as his son came into view. "You have no business here in the Dome. Go back to the tent, right now."

"I might ask the same of you, Father. No one comes to the Dome this time of night, much less alone. I want to know what's going on." His dark eyes were not friendly or kind, much like his father's. He had long suspected that his father was up to something. Tonight he had followed him in order to discover what it was.

"I'm not ready to tell you or anyone else. Now leave. And do not say anything to anyone about me being here. I will tell you when I'm ready."

"Very well," Oland pretended to agree. "I will await your timing." He turned to walk back to the door. He slid the door open, crouched low and slid the door almost closed, while remaining inside. He would stay hidden for a while to see if he could find out more. He watched as Brasald pulled the vials back out of the cabinet and continued his work, unaware his son watched quietly from behind a shelf.

Sometime later, as Brasald began to put away his experiments, Oland quickly slipped through the Dome's door and ran off towards the camps. He had heard enough as his father mumbled to himself to get some idea what the plans were. But for now he was not certain what he would do with his knowledge.

CHAPER FOUR

It was teaching time again and Damond, Eliot, Marna, and Sared, along with the other young people from both camps, were seated in the grass, the little ones who were old enough to attend classes sat in front of them. They were crowded close to Henric, one of the elders, eager to begin. After the class opening, Deblan, Last Companion of another elder, Conrand, and Janed, Henric's Companion would come to take the younger children for lessons that involved more activity. The two leaders, Vandlyn and Brasald maintained their camps slightly apart to give more room for hunting and cultivating fields for grain, but the young ones came together in the Unidan camp for teaching time and play. Through the years the Unidans had kept a closer allegiance to the ways of The One and the Originals, following the Covenant faithfully. Some of the Toldens had grown lazy in their pursuit of His ways and found it easier to send their young ones to the Unidan camp. Slowly but surely the lacks in the Tolden camp were beginning to show up in their young people.

This morning's chores were finished and much teasing had been aimed at Eliot for his extra water duty. As usual he was a good sport with it all and had pretended that he was not able to carry the load of water that Sared carried every day.

As they were laughing again at remembering his antics, Oland approached the group and sat to the side. It bothered the other young people that Oland seldom joined in their activities. He was different somehow and they were not sure why. He never really talked about The One as they did and they knew that his father did not see eye to eye with Vandlyn. But Oland was welcome if he desired to join them, although most of their overtures had gone without success over the years. Now and then when his anger flared, they felt the sting of his words. Only through speaking to The One were they able, most of the time, to keep from retaliating.

"Good morning, Oland," offered Marna. "It is good to see you this morning."

Oland ignored the offering and kept his eyes down, his face scowled as always. Just then Henric called for everyone's attention to begin the class. He spoke to The One and then began the day's opening recitation:

"Where is The One?" Henric asked the class, using one of several morning recitations.

"He is everywhere and within," chimed the youngest ones together.

"And whom is He within?" questioned Henric.

"Those who personally receive Him," came the chorus of little voices.

"And how does one receive Him?" Henric continued.

"By grace through faith," smiled the little ones.

"And what happens within?"

The Genesis of Atron

"We walk with Him as one!" everyone declared joyfully, finishing the morning's opening.

"Wonderful, children." Henric grinned at the young ones. "A good recitation."

As a group, they all closed their eyes to speak with The One within until Henric spoke the blessing, signaling the next part of class. "May The One have His way."

"And now Janed and Deblan will take you little ones for your reading and writing lessons," Henric continued, "while I continue with the young people. After that you can help make some baskets before playing tag and running races." The young ones jumped up, smiling and chattering to each other as they collected their packs containing wooden slates and chunks of charcoal. These were used in class as they began to learn to read, write and do math. As they grew older, they would learn to write on the Readers and while in the Dome they could use some of the Ancients' paper and writing tools. As the young ones happily followed the two women to the square, the older group drew closer to Henric--Oland remained separate and aloof.

A short time later, the day's teaching time came to an end. The older students prepared to leave for their Tazor practice before finishing various evening chores. Oland walked with the others towards the edge of the woods. Moving close to Damond and pretending to accidentally bump into him, he jabbed, "You think you know everything, don't you."

"What do you mean, Oland?" Damond responded stopping and turning towards him, looking him right in the eye.

Oland stared right back. "You don't know much of anything. There're big changes coming in this place and it will be soon. The Dome. . ."

"What about the Dome?" Damond stiffened, ready to defend himself if things escalated past talking.

"You'll have to wait and find out," Oland taunted as he turned to walk away, not finishing his sentence.

"Now what was that all about," Eliot wanted to know. "We've tried to include Oland many times and he won't join us or even give it a try. He seems angry all the time. What do you think he's talking about, Dame?"

Serad and Marna exchanged looks and said nothing. Damond poked Marna on the arm and said, "What?"

The girls looked at each other again. "We've heard some talk that it's not good in their tent. Brasald… well we don't want to say much. Something is going on at night after most of the camp is quiet. We saw Oland passing our tent towards the Tolden side very late last night. He was alone. But he is not the only one going and coming late at night."

"We've seen his father several times," added Serad. She looked down at the ground not sure what more to say.

"If they're doing something strange late at night then I think we should investigate and see what's going on," said Eliot, always ready for adventure. "We could follow him and then tell Father what we find out."

Damond began walking towards the forest edge again and the others followed him to the practice area. He leaned on the target stump and looked at Eliot. "Do you really think we should follow Brasald without telling Father?"

"Nothing's going to happen, Damond. We'll just follow him at a distance to see where he's going and then tell someone. It might be nothing. We would look foolish if we said something and it was nothing to get alarmed about."

"I'm with Eliot," Serad said. "It'll just be a little adventure with no harm to anyone."

"I don't know," Marna and Damond both said at the same time.

"Well, we two will do it without you then," Eliot volunteered throwing his arm across Serad's shoulder and grinning at her.

Damond looked at Marna with his eyebrows raised questioningly. She nodded. "I guess we'd better go along in case you two mess up and get into trouble," she said. "He hasn't been going until late. We'll all have to stay awake so we know when to leave. Let's meet here after everyone else is asleep and watch to see what they do tonight."

"I don't know about this," Damond replied once again doubtfully, "but I'll go along with it once. Then we're telling Father. Or I will tell him if I have to."

"This is great! A late-night adventure," Eliot said enthusiastically throwing his hands into the air. "I know we can pull it off and find out something if there is anything. Until then we don't say anything to anyone, alright?" Eliot reminded the others as he drew his Tazor. "Let's get in some practice."

CHAPTER FIVE

EARTHDATE June 2280

Father says we're nearing our destination. It's been a long, long weary trip. I'm so glad it's almost over. I'm so tired of being confined to this ship. I've adjusted some to the changes, but I'm still waiting for some adventures to begin. We have games to play and Readers to read or write in, but not much activity besides the workout rooms. The most fun we've had is playing hide and seek around the ship. Nik and I always hide from Tyra and Lisond, jumping out to frighten them when they pass our hiding place. We expect that landing on another planet in a different galaxy will certainly bring some adventure. And I haven't been as scared since we left. Getting away was difficult and we were almost caught right at the last moment. Father and the other men had made detailed plans. When they knew the ship was almost ready to take off for its colony, they began to smuggle items aboard that were not on the regular lists for a new colony, items such as The One's books and any others that would help them begin their new life under His ways.

When the time came to leave, the ten families who'd agreed to go had to come to the ship over a period of hours in order to avoid detection. We were waiting for the last family to arrive when we heard a loud commotion outside the fence. Father and Rondel ran to help. A guard had changed his course for some reason and seen the family using Father's card to enter the gate. While the family ran for the ship, Father and Rondel overpowered the guard and tied him up. The ship was primed and ready to leave when Father and Rondel fell through the hatch, slammed it shut and tightened the seal just as the ship left the ground. Everyone else was strapped in and Father and Rondel barely reached their seats before the ship left Earth's gravity. Nik and I were shaking by the time it was over and we were safe. No way did we want to do this adventure without our fathers. Everyone was so relieved to be on our way, thanking The One as we blasted off.

If not for the precise plans they'd made and the jobs they had at the colony shipyard, I don't think we could have pulled it off. Father and some of the others struggled greatly about taking the ship. The supplies being put on it were bound for another colony and our trip was unauthorized. But we had to go. Finally everyone agreed that the best way was to leave all their Credits and possessions behind to cover the cost. No one on Earth knows where we are going and most likely no one will take the trouble to find us.

Now we've been traveling these months and I can't wait to finally be on the ground again. They say we'll have to stay in the ship for a time as the planet is not quite habitable. Some of the vegetation and water will adapt to the changes we make to the air and weather with the MagnaRay. Father says there's not much wildlife other than some insects. All of us will have to work on the MagnaRay and the building to house it while we're wearing air suits. Once we get the building done, we can stay inside it until the air, vegetation and water are ready. Father says that it's very close to Earth's environment, but it'll take a little time to adjust everything with our instruments to make it right. It'll take a long time for the forests to thicken, but they've planned everything for how we'll eat and live until the land is ready. They say we'll be able to turn some of the animals loose before we can live outside all the time.

Do I ever know about those animals we brought with us from Earth! Remember I said we'd all have a part. Well, that's been mine-- I've had to help take care of them. They can really stink up the place. I'm thankful we have a good system for garbage and waste disposal— but somebody has to get it there and that's me. Nik helps. Ugh! Goats, pigs, sheep, chickens, bearcats, some birds and fish. . . plus what they

The Genesis of Atron

have stored in deep sleep or frozen eggs that they can bring back when it's time. I especially don't care for the bearcats as they've never been domesticated. They are ugly, smelly creatures, covered in scraggly brown fur, with large legs and round heads with fierce thin snouts filled with long yellow teeth. I don't think they are very intelligent, but they do make for good hunting and eating. They were bred by the scientists to be hunted by sportsmen, but Father says sometimes they were used for food in other countries. Anyway, we've got just what we need to keep the Covenant--to use as little technology as possible and live off the land. It's going to be a big change for all of us.

Father says when we finally move out for good that the tents we brought were made to never wear out. Although extremely light and easy to carry, the indestructible material makes it possible to cook inside the tents. The tents are part of the supplies for colonists traveling to new planets, making it possible to have instant shelter that's easily set up and easily taken down when necessary. That will enable us to move around as needed and not have to build permanent houses. We also brought Tazors, mostly because they were part of the package for all new colonies. I guess we'll use them for hunting. I can't see there being any war there in our new home.

It's a good thing that everything we brought with us for building the structure to house the MagnaRay --and the ray itself--works by sun power. But they say we're going to eventually live very simply as the Ancients did. I don't know how that will be, but I do know why the parents left. It was for us really, for their children. Not only would few people listen when we tried to tell them about The One and His ways, it became dangerous after the Electorate mandated that it was illegal to talk about The One, the Ancients and the old days. Father was blessed to have a job when the persecution grew worse and most of us who know The One became very cautious after some people were attacked or imprisoned for their beliefs. There were so few followers anymore and such little connection among the people and now open persecution. Our parents want to start over, fresh. It'll be fresh alright—nobody but us who are on this ship. Ten families, around fifty of us, on a whole new planet. I am very ready to be there, to get off this ship and to have something else to do. I'm glad we brought copies and Readers full of the Ancients' books and those of The One, but it will be good to have more activity and to be outside again.

Closing his reader, Damond expelled a deep breath as he lay back into his cushions and considered Eliot's push for some adventure for the night. *Maybe adventure is in our blood*, he thought. *Look at Jasend's family and the others. They risked everything to come here and begin a new life; to ensure that their children, and we, would know The One and His ways. Strange to give up all that's in the Dome, and all they knew before. But for me, I can't imagine anything else except the life I know-- a good life, with family and with The One.*

Damond's thoughts turned to the coming adventure. *But I do wonder what's going on with Oland and Brasald. Tonight maybe we'll see something and then we'll tell Father.*

As his family began to settle into their pillows and cloaks for the night Damond folded his arms under his head preparing to stay awake in order to meet the others. The fire was banked for the night and the camp was quiet. Soon he heard the even breathing that indicated his parents were asleep. But he and Eliot must wait a while longer to be sure that both camps were sleeping.

* * * * * *

"Damond," Eliot whispered shaking his brother's leg. "Let's go. It's time to meet Marna and Serad at the stump." Damond rolled over and sat up quietly, lacing his boots.

The boys slipped carefully out of the tent and walked to the stump. Marna and Serad were already there waiting. The four faded into the woods to a spot where they could watch for any movement coming from around the Tolden camp. It didn't take long before they saw Brasald leave his tent and find his way past the Unidan camp as he took the path towards the Dome. The adventurers gave him time to get ahead enough that he would not see them as they followed quietly at the edge of the path. The stars were showing and Atron's moon shed just enough light to guide their steps.

Four pairs of eyes observed Brasald opening the door to the Dome and slipping inside. Four pairs of eyes looked at each other with shock. What would anyone be doing in the Dome alone at night and without permission? "Let's get closer," Eliot said, taking a step in that direction. "We need to see what he's doing."

"No!" shushed Damond grabbing his arm. "We said one trip and that just to observe and then we would tell Father. That is all I agreed to. Now come on back to camp. Something big and bad is going on. We might have a part in helping, but not without Father."

"Damond is right," agreed Serad. "Yes, I wanted to do this, but I don't want to go any further. Come on Eliot. Let's go back."

"Oh, alright," came the reluctant reply. "Not much of an adventure to me, but I guess better than nothing for now." The four turned to retrace their steps back to their camp completely unaware that another pair of eyes had been watching them. Oland, on his way to spy on his father again had seen them in time to pause and listen to their reasons for being out. As they disappeared back towards camp, he moved closer to the Dome.

* * * * * *

The Genesis of Atron

By the soft glow of Atron's moon, Oland saw that his father had come outside the Dome. Oland crept closer through the trees to better see what his father was doing. Brasald walked slowly around the Dome and off into the field behind it. He was carrying something in his hands. Oland hugged the side of the Dome as he followed his father. In the field, his father raised up whatever it was in his hands and began to operate it. Oland saw a heavy, misty spray come from the object. The spray fell onto the plants within a large circle around Brasald as he slowly turned while operating the sprayer. He took the time to make several of these circles branching out from the field. When the sprayer was empty, Brasald turned to walk back to the Dome. Oland was not quick enough and his father saw him watching.

"What are you doing? I told you not to come around here! Get inside right now!"

Oland stomped to the Dome's door and went inside. He would demand that his father tell him what was going on. If not, he would go to Vandlyn, though that was the last thing he wanted to do. He wanted to be part of what was going on. He turned to glare at his father, fists clenched and fierce determination on his face.

"I saw you, Father. Tell me what you're doing or I'll go to Vandlyn."

"Don't you threaten me," growled Brasald. "I'm working on something to make a better life. I'm sick of all this work when magic lies within our reach here in the Dome. Vandlyn won't listen. He follows The One and the Covenant of the Originals. I will do what I wish and anyone who wants to go with me can decide that for themselves." Brasald stared at his son, waiting on a reaction.

"I'm with you, Father. Include me," he begged. "Let me help."

The Genesis of Atron

"I've made a liquid that will ensure our success. You saw me using it just now. It will make the plants grow faster and larger." Brasald eyes grew wider as he spilled his plan. "We can eventually move from the camp and have our own fields. Labor will be cut way back. We'll have time to explore. I will not have to share leadership with Vandlyn. We can do as we please." He could almost taste his desire as he continued. "No more living in camps—we will build a city!"

Oland was frightened but would not show it. "What do you want me to do?" he asked. This plan sounded extreme, not like anything he'd expected or knew, but the fear of his father's disapproval and wrath overrode his fear of the unknown, keeping him quiet. The desire for his father's approval and acceptance drove Oland far more than any fears. Brasald saved his annoyances and rejections for private moments like this one, seldom showing them in public, but Oland knew them well.

In addition to his father's cruelty, Oland had no mother to run to for comfort, something he ached for, but also had to hide. The aloneness he felt never eased up even when with the others his age. But he couldn't show any of this to anyone. No. Better to be tough and hard. He kept his body stiff and hid his fear as his father answered.

"For now, there is nothing you can do except stay out of my way. I must wait to see how the spray works in the field. Keep quiet and wait. No one else needs to know."

"I saw Vandlyn's boys watching the Dome tonight when you came."

"They must not tell Vandlyn. We have to stop them until I see the results, until I'm sure the formula works."

The Genesis of Atron

"That can be my part then," Oland offered eagerly. "I would like to show them who I am." Oland touched his Tazor as he spoke and smirked at his father.

"Very well. Stop them for a day or so and then I'll know about the formula. If it turns out as I planned, we'll be free to do as we please, free from the Covenant and others' leadership."

"You can count on me," Oland bragged. "I know just the way."

* * * * * *

The sun was barely showing over the horizon as Damond awoke, remembering the night's adventure. He had to talk to his father. It would not be easy to tell him that they had gone out last night to follow another person, especially a leader. Damond remembered well the lessons he'd had as a young one whenever he'd lied or taken something that didn't belong to him. These were serious offenses and the Unidan families treated them as such. The young ones had to own up to what they had done and talk to the person they'd offended. *Father was and is always kind and fair,* thought Damond as he rolled up his cloak and stacked his pillows to the side. *I remember that time I was supposed to work in the food garden and I went off to play in the forest instead. When Father asked me about it, I told him I was working. His face told me he knew otherwise. He told me how much he loved me and that I was not bad but what I did was wrong and that he and Mother would not tolerate lying in our family. I didn't have to encounter many of those lessons with him to get the message: it's not profitable to lie or to bother things that belong to other people.*

The One was using these memories from Damond's early lessons to prick his heart as he gave thought to approaching his father. There was no fear of his father, but there was the knowledge that his father would prefer he lived in the ways of The One and not do rash things.

Best thing to do is just to do it, Damond prodded himself. *I don't like to be out of joy with my father and I know we will work it out.*

"Eliot, I'm ready to talk to Father," Damond said quietly on their side of the tent. I hope you're going to be there with me.'

"Yes, I'm ready," Eliot turned from stacking his own pillows. "I know Father will know what to do and we really don't. Still it was exciting to go out like that even it was brief. Not dangerous, huh, just exciting."

"Sometimes exciting can turn dangerous, Eliot."

"Sure, sure, Brother, but I still like a little excitement now and then."

Damond didn't want to lecture his brother, but couldn't help remembering the thoughts he'd just had about their early lessons. "Father hasn't taught us to follow the ways of The One to keep us from having adventures, you know; it's for our good. Remember that time last winter when we were hunting and Father was almost killed by the boar? That was an adventure turned dangerous. Good thing he had his Tazor ready."

Eliot, always the optimist, paused to think before speaking again. "Well, I guess if you look at it that way, talking to Father right now could be seen as an adventure. We do need a bit of courage to confess and take what comes. And there is a taste of danger here since we have to tell him we went out and we don't know exactly what he'll do with us."

Eliot laughed nervously at his own evaluation. It would certainly not be a life and death type of danger. But that awe of Father could bring some very shaky feelings in the pit of one's stomach. "I know

Father will be fair, but three days of carrying Serad's water will seem to be a game if I know our father."

Damond laughed along with his brother. "As The One says, El, 'A father disciplines the sons that he loves.' And there is no doubt in my mind that Father loves us." The brothers straightened their shoulders, preparing to take what would come. Damond continued, "So there's no doubt we will have discipline. Let's do it and find out what 'adventure' we'll have as a result of the one last night."

Vandlyn and Amaz were working by the fire preparing the morning meal of eggs boiled in water. From the grain that the boys had gathered and ground, Amaz made flat, tasty cakes that would fill their stomachs for the day. There was goat's milk to drink, just retrieved from the cold stream, waiting in their cups. The parents had noticed first the whispering and then the nervous laughing on the other side of the tent, so they weren't surprised when the boys approached in a more serious mood.

"Father, we have something to tell you," Damond began as he sat down near the fire and food.

"I think I should do it, Dame, since it was my idea," Eliot interrupted as he also took his place for breakfast.

"What is it, boys?" Vandlyn asked as he handed each a plate of food. "You seem very serious this morning. Is it about last night?"

The boys looked with shock at each other and quickly turned to their plates, guessing that Father already suspected something. It was rather hard to get past him and they had learned at an early age that it was best not to try too often. All Unidan children were brought up in love, joy and kindness while being taught to respect and obey their parents and love themselves and others. Knowing The One and His ways was the center of life, the very reason they were on Atron. It made them who they are and shaped their values. Most of the people still held to these ways brought by the Originals. But after last night's observations, Damond was beginning to wonder if some in the Tolden camp might have wandered away from holding to His ways.

Eliot had volunteered to speak, so he continued humbly, looking up from his plate. "Yes, Father. It sounds like you know we went out. We didn't want to wake you. Thought we didn't. We wanted an adventure. I guess we're getting one now trying to tell you." He glanced at Damond before continuing. "Marna and Serad told us that they had seen Oland and Brasald out in the night. We decided to follow them if they did it again. We followed Brasald to the Dome."

"Uh, hum," Vandlyn mumbled as he chewed his wheat cake and glanced over at Amaz who was trying to be serious and keep from smiling at the same time while watching her boys confess.

"Brasald went into the Dome, Father," Damond took up the confession. "We had agreed to only find out where they were going and then tell you. We were tempted to follow further, but stuck to our original agreement. It was wrong to sneak out and we want your forgiveness for that." Damond looked his father in the eye as he spoke. "Will you forgive us? We accept your discipline."

Eliot chimed in with the same question and awaited their father's replies. Vandlyn looked at Amaz who nodded her agreement, confirming that they had already discussed this situation. "You are forgiven. Mother and I will decide what to do about the sneaking out part of it and tell you later. For now, we'll talk about our thoughts on what might be going on. You boys are getting old enough to be included."

"Thank you, Father," the boys said at the same time. Damond continued for both, "We know you have to handle what we saw. We want to help if we can."

As they all finished the meal, Vandlyn spoke to The One in thanksgiving for their food and for wisdom in this situation with Brasald. Then he spoke to the boys. "I've been concerned for some time that Brasald was up to something, but I do not know what. You've confirmed that it involves something in the Dome. I'm going to speak to Brasald and confront him. It might not go well. He has become a stubborn and angry man; it seems he may not wish to follow The One. There's much to be decided and I will need some of the other men to help me. We'll talk of it later."

The family stirred from their seats around the fire to go about their chores. There was water to haul and grain to gather. There were animals to feed and care for. There were classes to attend and friends to talk with. Damond and Eliot wondered how the girls had fared with their father and mother. And—what would his and Eliot's discipline be for disobeying.

CHAPTER SIX

EARTHDATE July 2280

We're here! We landed yesterday with no problems. I can see through some of the portals that the land has some trees, but with barren places, not like a desert, just not much vegetation. They say the air is almost good enough, but we will have to work in suits until the MagnaRay is working. I'll have to continue to take care of the animals until everything is ready. It's still not my favorite job but Nik and I manage and the waste gets incinerated instantly. We're very thankful for that piece of technology that we didn't have to leave behind. The adults are unloading the equipment to build a dome. They say that will work the best to house everything and manage the MagnaRay. Without the MagnaRay, we wouldn't be able to stay here. It will make the seasons we're used to, control the rain, help the plants and cleanse the water that's here. The seasons will be mild but changeable. I'm glad of that.

The tents we'll use are something else. There are different sizes with some big enough for a family and others right for one, two or three people. They say we won't be able to reproduce the material they're made of for very long. I wonder if we'll ever go back to houses and cities. They say not. At least we'll have our Readers and Tazors. Mother says we'll use some things from the ship for medicine and research. And of course we'll have classes and be able to study the books of The One and the Ancients. There will also be a lot of work to do in order to eat and live, so I don't think there's any danger of being bored.

I best stop writing for now and see what's next. I'm ready to go out even if I have to wear a suit. Nik and I get to go soon, our fathers said yesterday.

As he looked up from Jasend's diary, having taken a break out by the stream to read for a while after the evening meal, Damond thought about that time so long ago when Jasend and the others came to Atron. He knew from previous readings that Nik was Jasend's close friend and Tyra and Lisond were Nik's sisters. Jasend's father Atlan and Nik's father, Rondel, were the principle leaders of the quest for a new colony. They had worked together in the industry for colonizing other planets and had followed The One faithfully even when it was very unpopular. When the persecution worsened, it was they who had finally decided enough was enough and put together the plan to leave.

Each had carefully discussed with other families who followed The One if they would be interested in leaving. There they found the other willing families.

The Electorate on Earth allowed families to colonize other planets under their rule. But there were many regulations and much pressure to become like Earth, with ships going and coming regularly to assure compliance. Electorate mandates were not what Atlan and Rondel wanted for their families. Thus taking the ship and its supplies, leaving behind their possessions and Credits to cover the cost, the ten families fled without permission. No one knew where they had gone. Most likely no one would care to search and they would be free. From these two fathers, Atron got its name. From these families, Unidans and Toldens descended. *And here in my time,* Damon thought, *we still hold the Covenant and follow The One Within.*

Damond heard a sound that interrupted his thoughts. The scrape of a boot on the rocks caused him to look up as Oland stepped into his line of sight. *I wonder what he wants,* thought Damond. *He seldom comes around us like he did yesterday. Always seems angry. Won't interact with us or join our games or work with us in the fields.*

"Hey, Damond. Sorry about yesterday. I was looking for you and your friends. Thought we might get in a little extra Tazor fun before dark. You interested?"

"Sure, Oland. I'll call the others." Damond stood to his feet and stretched after his drowsy time on the ground. "You want to wait or meet us at the stump?"

"I'll wait," he said shifting from one foot to the other, hand on his Tazor. He watched as Damond went to their tent to put away his Reader and ask Eliot to get the girls. They converged by the stream where Oland was waiting and everyone strapped on their Tazors while

The Genesis of Atron

Marna grabbed a hide that they could use to cover the stump. The sun was moving towards the end of the day, but there was yet enough light to take a few shots and parries. Not many were out in the camps as preparation for the coming night drew them inside.

The young people arrived at the stump and began to decide how they would divide up since they had an uneven number. Oland was paired with Sared, with Eliot and Marna together. Damond would watch as they practiced and decide who would change out next. They each fired a few light bursts first, covering the hide with black ashes. Then they paired off for some sword practice. Oland, who was bigger and stronger than Sared, began to move on her aggressively. She was faltering when suddenly Oland knocked her Tazor to the ground and pointed the tip of his Tazor right at her chest. Sared froze.

Hearing the Tazor hit the ground, the others turned to look. They could not believe what they were seeing.

"Don't any of you move or I will hurt her," Oland ordered the others before they could move. "Put down your Tazors and your Sedats, right now."

Eliot and Marna laid down their Tazors, never taking their eyes off of Oland and Sared. Damond unsheathed his, debating inside if there was anything he could do. But he had no precedence for what to do when someone was pointing a Tazor at another's chest. Sensing from The One that he should do as Oland ordered, he carefully laid down his Tazor. All four removed their Sedats, placing them on the ground.

"Now, Sared, turn and go through the woods there away from the camps."

Sared turned slowly while Oland kept his Tazor point close to her body, aiming it at her back after she turned. "Everyone else, get up

2009 Barbara Moon

there in front of Sared so I can see you." The others obeyed as the group began to move through the woods.

"Go straight until I tell you to turn," their captor demanded. The four marched quietly without talking or looking at each other. They were extremely frightened for Sared and did not want to take any chances with Oland's anger. It was getting dark when they heard Oland speak again. Atron's moon was covered with clouds and the sun was almost gone.

"Now turn to the right through that clearing and keep going until I tell you." After several more minutes, they barely made out what must be their destination—a cave that they had never seen before. "Go on," growled Oland. "Get in there."

Inside they found that Oland had made preparations for their visit. There were hide ropes, some cloaks and some water. "Tie up the others, Damond," ordered Oland, "and you better do a good job of it or she gets hurt."

Damond moved to obey, using the hide to tie both Eliot's and Marna's hands in front of their bodies. He then tied their ankles. Again he debated a way to overpower Oland, but seeing the point of that Tazor touching Serad's chest was all he needed to continue obeying Oland's demands.

"Now hers," Oland said pointing at Serad.

"What are you trying to prove?" Damond dared to ask as he moved to tie Serad beside the others.

"No talking! You're going to stay here until tomorrow so you can't talk to your father. I saw you in the woods last night watching my father. You are not going to stop him. Neither will your father. I told you things were going to change. This is just the beginning. Now sit down there with the others and if you try anything, I will still hurt her."

Damond sat down beside Eliot while Oland tied his hands and feet. He was not about to tell Oland that it was too late—that their father knew something was going on and was ready to confront Brasald. *Father will find us,* he thought, *and The One is with us right now. He glanced at the others and saw that they were afraid but not terrified. It would seem that all four of them were talking with The One within. They would cooperate and not take a chance on escalating Oland's anger.* Damond tried to encourage the others with a look as Oland bent to check all the ropes.

"After my father has finished what he's doing, I'll return and let you go. By then it won't matter anyway. His plans will be well under way." Oland gave them one more angry look as he turned to walk away. "Soon you will see who's the best around here."

"Is everyone alright?" Damond asked as soon as Oland was out of sight. The others nodded uncertainly, rightfully worried about how the next few hours would feel. Damond moved over to Eliot and tried to loosen the knots he had tied earlier, but it was no use. The hide was too strong.

The sun went down past the trees, extinguishing the remaining light filtering into the cave.

* * * * * *

Vandlyn was speaking with The One as he prepared to go and talk with Brasald. It was not going to be easy. Vandlyn already knew from experience that Brasald was hard to disagree with. *But I have waited long enough*, Vandlyn mused as he conversed with The One, hearing

The Genesis of Atron

His assurance. '*It's time. The children are involved. I will speak through you.*' He rose and left the tent, walking towards the Tolden camp. He found Brasald stacking some firewood beside his tent.

"A moment with you, Brasald?"

Brasald set down the stack of wood he had just split and moved to the stream to wash his hands. The two men sat down near the tents-- Vandlyn got right to the point. "I understand that you've been going to the Dome sometimes at night. I have to ask you what you're doing. It's not part of the Covenant from the Originals."

Discomfort flickered across Brasald's face, quickly replaced by determination. He chose his words carefully but firmly. "I no longer hold to the Covenant, Vandlyn. I do not want to live as we do here any longer. I want to separate from your camp and go my own way. I will take with me whoever wants to go along."

"This does not surprise me," Vandlyn replied as he met Brasald's eyes, "but it deeply saddens me. Brasald looked down as Vandlyn continued, "What about The One?"

"The One is The One. I will go my way, He will go His."

Vandlen's heart grieved to hear such a statement from his old friend. His suspicions were true. Brasald was not the person he had pretended to be all these years. Vandlen felt tricked and betrayed—and a bit stupid. But he would deal with that later with The One. For now he had another question. "What are you doing at the Dome?"

"I've been doing experiments to help me with my new plans. I've made a formula that will grow plants bigger and faster. It will change the makeup of the plants. I've already tested it and I know it works. There is nothing you can do about it. It will make life a lot easier and as my plan unwinds, I'll be able to build a city and have time for other things beside dirty, hard work. I'm taking things from the Dome to make our lives a lot easier."

"I do not like this at all, Brasald. It goes against everything the Originals came here for. It goes against the ways of The One. Does that not alarm you at all?"

"No," came the emphatic reply. "It's what I want to do. You can't stop me."

"I will continue to try to dissuade you, you know. I owe that to The One and our people." Vandlyn rose to leave, his shoulders slumped and his face downcast with the change in his friend. It was worse than he thought. How could he have not seen it coming a long time ago? *Brasald hid it well,* he thought as he walked the path back to Unidan. *What do I do now, Most High One*, he spoke within. *What steps do I take to protect the Covenant, the other people, the Dome?* Vandlyn's heart was heavy. *I must speak with Amaz and some of the other elders and listen to You.*

Upon reaching the edge of the Unidan camp, Vandlyn paused and released a deep sigh of sadness. It was growing dark and it occurred to him that he did not see any of the young people about. Damond was usually reading while Eliot entertained Marna and Serad with his antics. He looked inside the tent to make sure they were not there. Amaz was just stooping to light the oil lamps and looked up as she heard the rustle at the doorway. "How did it go, Love?" she inquired as she blew out her lighting straw.

"It was as I expected," answered Vandlyn. "I will tell you later. Where are the boys?"

The Genesis of Atron

"They headed for the practice stump a while back. They should have been here by now. It's nearly dark." A touch of alarm sounded in her voice.

"I'll go there to check," said Vandlyn as he turned and hurried from the tent. Right up against the woods he saw the practice stump with its darkened hide hanging over the top. But he saw no young people. *But wait, what's that beside the stump?* he asked himself as he ran closer. *Oh, No!!* He stooped to the ground. *What's going on? Why are their Tazors and Sedats here on the ground? They know better than that. They never go anywhere without their Tazors.*

Vandlyn picked up the four Tazors and Sedats and ran back to Marna and Serad's tent, yelling for Amaz and the girls' parents as he approached both tents. The other parents met him at the path. "Have you seen the children? I found their Tazors by the target stump. I can't tell anything by the prints around there."

"We know they left together a while back as the sun was lowering," answered Conrand with unease in his voice. He took two of the Tazors and quickly nodded that those were his girls'.

"What shall we do?" asked Amaz as she and Deblan held each other's hands. These kinds of things seldom happened in the camps.

"Let's speak to The One aloud," said Vandlyn as he looked at each of the others' concerned faces. "O, One, we come to You for wisdom and comfort. We do not know where our children are at this hour when all are usually together for the night. What would You have us do?"

As the parents listened within, Amaz spoke that she was sensing The One's assurance that He was taking care of the children. "There's no way we can search in the dark past where our voices would reach;

we don't even know which direction to begin. We'll have to wait until sunrise," she said with a catch in her voice, "and trust The One."

"Why doesn't He just tell us where to find them?" asked Deblan anxiously. And then as she sensed His peace, she answered her own question—"I know, I know--so we will trust Him." She managed to smile at her friends and waited for the joint decision.

"Let's spread the word around the camps and see what we can find out from any others," Vandlyn said as he checked each face for agreement. "We'll get everyone to speak to The One and as soon as the first light begins to show we'll spread out in all directions." *And, he wondered to himself, does this have anything to do with Brasald's plans. While we have everyone together, I should go ahead and speak to the other leaders about that situation. I don't think any of us are going to get much sleep tonight.*

* * * * * *

"My arms hurt," said Serad as she squirmed to find a better way to sit trussed up in the cave.

"At least he left us some water," said Marna as she struggled to take a sip with both hands tied together. The four had been in the dark for quite a while and were finding it very difficult to think about sleeping. Their spirits were fair, all things considered, as they talked to The One aloud and within, talked to each other and trusted that The One and their parents would take care of the situation.

"I believe the people will wait until morning to look for us," Damond mused. "There isn't much they can do in the dark when they don't know where to begin. We're too far away to yell. We'll have to listen at first light for their calling so we can answer."

The Genesis of Atron

"What do you think the elders will do with Oland?" Eliot asked. He was not quite as full of fun as usual as he thought about spending the night in a cave far from home with no fire or oil lamps for light. The moon was again obscured behind some clouds and was not any help to either group—the lost or the searchers.

Damond was not sure how to answer that question as nothing like this had ever happened on Atron. Most all disagreements were easily settled and there had never been a thought of anyone taking someone else somewhere by force. Father and the elders would have to decide with The One. *And what will be the result of Father's talk with Brasald when they know of Oland's deed being added to the mix?* he thought to himself. *I think Oland is right about one thing though— some things are really going to change around here.*

"Father and the elders will know, Eliot," Damond finally said after thinking about Eliot's question. "Right now I think we should try to get some sleep if we can lean on each other and cover ourselves with these cloaks somehow. We'll need strength in the morning.

As everyone squirmed to get more comfortable, Damond continued, "We could talk about when Jasend and Nik arrived and the Originals began to build the Dome and how their story progressed. It'll help us pass some time and then maybe we'll be able to sleep. What do you think? Everyone can fill in the story."

"Good idea, Dame, since we're a captive audience here so to speak," Eliot said trying to manage a little fun. "You start."

"I like the part where Jasend and Nik go outside the ship for the first time in their suits. It sounds like they had a lot of laughs encasing themselves from head to toe and then seeing how strange they looked. Jasend says that they sounded odd to each other, too, through their speakers. I can't imagine how bulky it would feel to walk around like

The Genesis of Atron

that after being in space for months. They were so glad to get out, I guess they didn't care. They walked around and looked at the place where the parents had marked off for the Dome. It was going to be huge."

Damond paused to remind the others of the many times they'd played around the Dome. "You know it took us a long time to run all the way around it when we used to play out there. And the door is as tall as two men and as wide as five. It's still something I like to do now and then—walk all the way around it."

"I do, too," added Marna. "Sometimes I go there to talk with The One. The walk around it is just right for a break from my chores."

"I like to go inside," said Sared. "There is so much to look at and explore and think about. Sometimes Father shows me his research about the Ancients and the Originals. It's fun to taste the Instameals and explore the old living quarters."

"Do you ever wish we could use more of the technology for everyday living?" Eliot asked into the darkness.

"I do wonder about it sometimes," Damond answered aloud as the girls murmured their agreement. "But I try to remember the Covenant and the reasons we're here on Atron. I wouldn't trade all the technology in the world for knowing The One and the love we have in our families."

"I'm glad we have the Readers and all the books," Eliot said. "And the medicine," he added. "I guess it was difficult for the Originals to come up with good compromises without going against their reasons for coming here. I'm not going to complain, though I do think about it now and then. But following The One without fear is worth any sacrifices."

"Well said, El," Damond agreed. "Now I'll go back to my story about when Jasend and Nik were looking at the Dome's future location."

"Jasend said his father told him it would work better for the MagnaRay to be set up in a dome. On most new colonies that was the plan, plus it gave lots of room for the families to live inside until they could move outside for good." Poking Eliot, Damond encouraged him to take up the tale.

"My favorite part is when they began to figure out how to use the Tazors," Eliot began to no one's surprise, "the time when they learned the secret. I can just see them now making a light blast when they had not pushed the red buttons. Good thing it was not pointed at anyone. Jasend and Nik were playing around with one of their targets and Jasend was speaking to The One about his shot and suddenly it blasted right at the target before he pushed the button. Didn't it take them a few more trials before they made the association to The One?"

"Yeah, that was a little later when it happened to one of the parents, if I remember correctly," added Marna. Continuing the story, she said, "I think about how they lived and ate before the animals grew and multiplied and they could hunt for meat. Do you think they got tired of the Instameals in the Dome? Personally I like what Mother cooks for us better, but I can see why the Earth people would like the convenience." Marna scooted closer to Serad, fumbling in the dark to pull one of the cloaks over their legs in spite of having her hands tied. The night was cooling and the cave was almost cold now.

Serad took up the tale as she reminded the others of the discovery of what came to be called Waters Mountain. "I can only wonder what the Originals thought when they first explored the mountain. And how long did it take them to discover the mystery of the water? As far as we know there's nothing like it anywhere else on Atron, or where they came from either. The changes in the water are amazing and to see the changes we have to know the exact time and season. I am in awe each time we go there."

"That's one of my favorite travels," Marna agreed. "Father and Mother like to go each time it's to occur. Of all that the MagnaRay does to control our weather, Waters Mountain is solely of Atron—and The One. What a wondrous sight it is. And the underwater plants are more vibrant than any plants I've ever seen."

Marna sighed deeply, her exuberance dying. It was hard to keep their minds on other things besides the discomfort and fright of being tied up in a cold cave in the middle of the night. The group grew quiet as if to come up with some other distractions to their plight.

"Let's rest now," Damond suggested as he moved closer to Eliot to conserve warmth, pulling the other cloak over their arms. "The One is here within. Father will come. The sun will rise."

The other young people reluctantly murmured agreement and settled closer to each other awaiting the dawn. Though they felt scared and anxious, they knew that The One was with them and that their parents would search until they were found. Sadness for Oland stirred in their hearts, but what would happen to him was not their problem to solve. The elders would do that. As they settled, each whispered softly to The One, Marna began to sing a song of The One and they tried to sleep.

* * * * * *

Oland was far away from the cave where he had left the others. Now that he had made it happen, he was sure his father would praise his accomplishment as soon as he knew about it. *For now I'll stay hidden here on the other side of the Dome, as far from the camps as I* can get. *The others' parents will be frantically searching for them and by the time they're found, hopefully my part in the event will be less important than what Father is doing and I won't have to pay. I knew some day this small tent I hid here would be useful. I can hold out here for a couple of days. Not unusual. Father doesn't pay attention and no one else cares.* Oland closed his eyes, thinking only of how clever he had been and how he was helping his Father. He had tried many things to get that approval and with luck, this time it would work. He slept.

* * * * * *

Atron's sun rose over the horizon and struck the top of the Dome, bouncing colors of every hue back to the clear sky, breaking open the morning. Right on time, the MagnaRay sent forth its purple streak of intense light into the atmosphere. The four young people's parents stirred quickly to eat some food and gather with others from the camps to plan their search. They would go in all directions, carrying food and water, calling out as they covered more and more ground until they received a response or found something. If anyone found anything, they would use their Tazor as a flare by shooting it into the air.

Vandlyn and Amaz had been walking south to southwest of the Tolden camp for some time calling their boys' names. The last echo of "Daaaamonnnnd" had not quite ended when Amaz grabbed Vandlyn by his arm, "I heard something! Over that way," she pointed to her right. They broke into a run, straining to hear any sound that would help them find their children. "I heard it again, Vandlyn! Hurry!"

"Heeellllpp!" came the scream of four loud voices not too far ahead.

"Daamond, Elioott, we're here. Keep yelling!" At last Vandlyn and Amaz broke through the trees and saw the cave. The most wonderful sight they'd ever beheld was right in front of them. All four

The Genesis of Atron

young people, having scooted outside the entrance of the cave, were yelling at the top of their voices while sitting there bound hand and foot. Vandlyn raised his Tazor and shot a long blast into the morning sky to signal the other searchers that they had found the children. All thoughts of discipline for going out the night before fled from his thoughts with the relief at finding the young people as The One had said.

"We knew you would come," they all began to talk at once. "The One was with us. It helped to talk with Him."

"I'm starved."

"I'm thirsty."

"Help me get loose. We tried to loosen each other but the knots were too tight."

"I don't know if I can walk."

Vandlyn and Amaz drew their Sedats and stooped to cut the stubborn knots. Relief brought the tears that they'd held in check all through the night. Amaz hugged the girls first and then her boys. Vandlyn took out his water and everyone drank thirstily.

"I've never tasted such delicious water," Eliot said as he wiped his arm across his mouth. "We drank all that was here. We're so glad to see you."

"And we the same," answered his father as he leaned over to give Eliot another hug. "What happened? Who did this to you?" Vandlyn looked from one to the other as the young people questioned each other with their eyes.

2009 Barbara Moon

The Genesis of Atron

"It was Oland, Father," said Damond. "He tricked us last night and threatened to hurt Serad if we didn't do as he said. He said he was coming back after his father finished some plans he was making. Is this part of what we saw the other night? What's going on?"

"We will decide later what to do about Oland," Vandlyn answered. "I only had time last night to talk briefly to the elders. We'll certainly be talking again. I'll include you in the telling. But for now, let's get everyone back to the camp so Conrand and Deblan will know their girls are alright. See how your legs feel," he reminded the young people as they began to try to stand and walk. After a few minutes of hobbling around, they were ready to go back to camp. Amaz handed each one a cake and some cheese. Everyone drank from the hides of water again.

* * * * * *

The camps had settled after the safe return of the young people and all the searchers. The parents had thanked both camps for their assistance in the search. No one had seen Oland or Brasald and for the moment did not want to. After gathering by the stream to thank The One before dispersing for morning chores, Vandlyn had told the Unidan elders that he was calling a council in the afternoon so that they could discuss the situations of the last few days. Now, as the sun lowered, the elders entered Vandlyn's tent and took seats upon the cushions that surrounded the banked fire, greeting Damond and Marna who were already present; Brasald and his people were obviously absent. Vandlyn began by describing his concerns, what the young people had observed and his decision to confront Brasald.

"I do not yet know all that he has planned," Vandlyn said, "but I do know he's set on turning from the Covenant and going his own way with whoever wants to follow him. He has been experimenting with some chemicals from the Dome. He's told me he no longer wants to follow The One's ways. And that he's going to take things from the Dome when he leaves."

Conrand spoke quietly as Vandlyn paused. "It seems to me that we must secure the Dome. We must do all we can to protect the Covenant and see no misuse of the Dome's contents."

"I agree," replied Vandlyn as he looked from one to the other. "That's what I've been thinking. I wanted Damond and Marna here as representatives of the future of Atron. If all of us agree, I want to make a different way to lock the Dome and hide the new electrokey. I will make a map of where it's hidden and that map will be kept in our family until this crises passes."

Henric nodded, adding his opinion. "I sense from The One that we must move our camp as well, farther away from the Dome and farther from Brasald and his plans. It goes against all that we've done since the Originals. Everything that's happened is unlike anything we've seen before."

"I see we're all thinking in the same direction, Henric." Vandlyn continued, "The Unidan camp can prepare to move. I will work on redesigning and hiding the key and making the map. We must keep Brasald from taking anything else from the Dome or doing more experiments. He has what he's already made. We can't stop that."

"What about Oland, Father," Damond reminded his father.

"I think we'll just leave Oland to his father for now. I am sorry for what he did to you, but it appears that our camps are no longer united and under equal leaders."

"Whatever you say, Father. I am honored to be here with the council today. I want to do whatever you need me to do."

The Genesis of Atron

"And I as well," added Marna. "I'm here to help."

"It will take much work and preparation to move so we'll need everyone's help. Let's be ready as quickly as possible. I'll try talking to Brasald one more time." Vandlyn rose from the cushions and the others followed. All left the tent except Vandlyn, Damond and Amaz.

"I need for you to make a large parchment, Amaz. Do you have any ideas of how to make it?"

"Yes, I do. I will use some of the material from the Dome and sew it together to make it larger. I will get it ready."

"And I'll use some of the ink from the Dome to assure that the directions to the electrokey won't fade."

Vandlyn turned to Damond.

"Damond, much of this is going to be on your shoulders. Because of the events since last night, I am giving you grace on the issue of sneaking off. There's too much else to be looking at right now. It's my hope, that at the worst, within your generation our people can return to the Dome."

Vandlyn laid his hand upon his son's shoulder, looking right into his eyes. "This is a sad time for our people. Breaking the Covenant is serious--turning from The One even more so. Many things will change and we don't know all that's going to happen. It will mean much to have you by my side. You'll go with me to hide the key and you'll help me with the map. Neither Brasald nor any of his people can know where the key is and the parchment must be protected at all costs. Do you understand, Son?"

Damond's eyes reflected the seriousness that he heard from his father's words and saw on his face. This responsibility was more in line for a young man who had had his Becoming Day—the ceremony that marked the end of schooling and the beginning of adulthood. In ordinary times, that would be some three years away. But ordinary was no more since following Brasald to the Dome that night.

This must be how Jasend and Nik felt when their parents told them they would be leaving Earth, Damond thought as he glanced from his father over to his mother. *But these are not words in a Reader. This is real and like nothing I've ever had to live through before. How will I do it? What will it be like to move away from the Dome?* Damond saw his mother's resolve and strength as she stood with her head high, touching his father's arm. It was not an unusual sight, though the situation was new. *It's The One Within,* he thought without having to ask. *That's how they'll do it, how we all will do it.*

"I understand, Father. I feel scared but I know The One is with us. I know you will be with us, too."

"I'm proud of you, Son. I'm going to the Dome right now to make a new electrokey and a new lock for the Dome. When I return, we'll make the map. I know where I want to hide the key and we'll make the map in such a way that it will be difficult to follow. May The One have His way."

CHAPTER SEVEN

Oland had been hiding for three nights. His food was running low and he was anxious to see how his plan had worked out for his father. The sun was breaking through the early morning clouds as he sat up and turned out his pack to see what food he had left. *I think it's about time to go back,* he thought as he failed to find more than a small piece of cheese and some dried meat. *I can almost hear the praise from*

Father's lips after I've told him what I did to give him some time. I'm sure someone found the others the next morning. I know Vandlyn would not rest until he did. And I saw some of the other Unidans pass this way calling their names. I've no fear of what might happen to me as Father will be so proud. Yes, it's time to go back.

Oland began to unhook his tent preparing to crawl out. He could not get the hooks to come loose. "What?" he said aloud. Using as much force as he could muster, he jerked on the top hook. It came loose, but attached to it was a large vine like none Oland had ever seen before. He peered out of the hole in the tent door and jumped back in terror, falling to the floor of the tent, scrambling backwards as far as he could get. A piece of the vine was weaving itself towards the opening in the tent, and the whole tent and the area around it were covered with more of the large vines, their tendrils wound around the tent all the way to the top, with several going up into the trees around it.

How could this be? Nothing grows like that on Atron, he thought, his eyes round and full of fright. *I don't know if I can get out. What is this? It wasn't there yesterday.* Panic was setting in. *I have to get out.*

Oland drew his Tazor from its sheath and stuck it cautiously out the hole in the door. He tapped the red button, sending a light burst at one of the vines to see what it would do. It cut the vine cleanly, dropping it to the ground. He quickly cleared the door, picked up his pack and began clearing a path towards the Dome.

I have to find Father! Is this part of what he was doing the other night? I saw him spraying near here. I must find him! Shortly, Oland passed by the end of the vine and was able to run towards the camps. No longer excited about hearing praise for his deed with the Unidans, finding his father was his only thought.

CHAPTER EIGHT

As planned, The Unidan camp began preparations to move. Belongings had to be sorted and packed. The men had to make sturdy sleds and wagons to carry the belongings. Everyone would gather as much grain as possible and store it in bags. The precious seeds needed for new planting would be wrapped in protective cloths and hides. The children would herd the animals that could not be caged and tents would be folded at the last minute, placing them within easy reach beside other articles needed for camping as they traveled. A few Toldens wanted to come with the Unidans, but most wished to stay with Brasald. The choice was up to them.

Vandlyn had gone to Brasald again hoping to convince him to change his direction away from The One and the Covenant, but to no avail. When told what Oland had done with the other children, Brasald did not seem to care one way or the other. Vandlyn did not know what to think of the changes in his old friend. Apparently, Brasald had hidden his true feelings for years.

As the Undians prepared to move, Brasald watched disdainfully. All the better for his plans to use the Dome. Now he could do other experiments to help make his plans come true. He'd not been back to the Dome for a while, since he no longer had to hide what he was doing, and he had a bit of the orange spray stored in his tent. He'd kept an eye on the places he'd sprayed and had seen some quick growth. *It's no matter to me that they're going,* he thought as he watched the Unidans busily working. *I can build my city here if it pleases me. It might take some time to get far enough ahead, but I have all the time in the world to see my little kingdom grow.*

As he continued up the path past the Unidan camp Brasald gave a fleeting thought to his son. *Now where is that boy? He's been gone since the other children were lost. Oh, well, he'll turn up sooner or later. I've got more important things to do than worry about him and his antics.* Brasald turned towards the Dome thinking he would check his plants and make another batch of the formula. Off in the distance he saw Oland running as fast as he could towards the Undian camp.

As Oland neared, Brasald heard him shouting, "Father, Father! It's terrible! I was almost killed!"

"What are you babbling about now, Oland? Where have you been? I heard what you did to Vandlyn's boys."

"I did what you told me to—I stalled Vandlyn from knowing your plans," Oland panted. "Then I hid behind the Dome to let some time pass so I wouldn't get in trouble. But, Father, that's not why I'm here." Oland tried to calm himself. "The vines. . . They were all over the tent. I couldn't get out the door. . ."

"Whatever are you saying, Boy? What vines? What tent? Where?"

"Behind the Dome. The vines are huge, covering my tent, moving towards me, climbing up high into the trees. They weren't there yesterday!"

Brasald's body stiffened and his eyes grew large and round. *The experiments! It has to be the experiments,* he realized. "Show me now, Oland. Where? Take me there right now!"

All thoughts about the departing Unidans and any kind of discipline for his son, swiftly fled Brasald's mind when he heard Oland's description of the vines. The two turned, running quickly back towards the Dome.

As they rounded the northern side of the Dome, Oland halted in his steps and pointed, not wanting to go any closer. Brasald slowed to a walk upon seeing what Oland was pointing out. It was a mass of huge vines twisting and turning high into the trees covering what could barely be distinguished as a small tent. The leaves were as large as a man's chest and blooms were growing here and there that were big enough to cover a man. *This is not what I expected!* Brasald thought. *It has to be the formula. This is the area where I sprayed. I noted some quick growth the first and second night, but this? Way beyond what I was aiming for. I'll have to think about what to do. Change the formula a little?* Brasald continued to walk cautiously around the edge of the vine, evaluating the situation while Oland watched from a distance. *I have to go to the Dome right now and reformulate the liquid. It's too strong. This growth is much larger and extremely faster than I thought. I need something to slow it down, to regulate it. . .*

"Go back, Oland. Stay away from here. I'm going to the Dome to work." Brasald shoved Oland in the direction of the camps and headed for the Dome's door. "The Undians are preparing to move and everything will be different now. Vandlyn confronted me and tried to dissuade my plans. But I won't be stopped."

"Don't you want to know how I helped, Father? You wanted me to help you," Oland whined.

"Vandlyn told me what you did and I don't care. Nobody cares what you did. When I want your help again I'll ask you. Now go find something to do while I work at the Dome. We have a problem here that I've got to fix."

Oland's chin drooped to his chest. He felt shamed from his father's rejection, but that feeling quickly turned to anger as he clenched his fists, fighting the desire to retaliate. But he knew better. He turned to run away, hearing his father shout as he began to run, "And you'd better not mention anything about this vine to anyone else!"

Running past the busy Unidan camp, stumbling in his rage, Oland fled down the path to the Tolden camp and into his own tent.

* * * * * *

The Unidans were ready to leave. While the camp was finishing the last days' preparations, Vandlyn and Damond had traveled to Waters Mountain to hide the electrokey. The old lock, which was seldom used, was coded with numbers and letters. There had never been an occasion to worry about the use of the Dome as people had scheduled assignments for using the Dome wisely. There were no reasons to go there in the night. After his unsuccessful talks with Brasald, Vandlyn had worked swiftly to lock it as soon as possible.

Unknown to Brasald and using some of the technology in the Dome, Vandlyn had constructed a new and different key that would stay charged indefinitely, be activated by the sun at anytime and be ready to open the Dome when properly used. It was stored tightly in a case similar to the covers on the Readers. The case was indestructible and waterproof. The new lock on the Dome's door was now invisible to the naked eye. The only way to find the lock on the door was to have the new electrokey in close proximity to the lock. The lock would then glow.

While his father had been finishing the lock and key, Damond had made the last entry in the Dome's report log, leaving a small duplicate drawing of the parchment map they'd made and bringing the log up to date with an explanation of their reasons for leaving, not knowing when anyone would read it again. Amaz had sewn together some material from the Dome and after returning to the camp from their journey to the mountain, Vandlyn and Damond had worked into the night to finish the map, masking as best they could the exact path to the key. The markings showed the big river, the mountain and the Dome, all disguised as scribbling interspersed with riddles. A smaller version that showed the way to the Dome from the hiding place had been hidden with the electrokey. Anyone but a true follower of The One would find it difficult to translate the marks and riddles.

At this time, only Vandlyn, Damond and Amaz knew where the key was hidden. They planned to keep the parchment map hidden among their possessions in case the people were unable to return to the Dome in a short time. Vandlyn, trying to plan for various scenarios, had accepted that any further attempts to change Brasald's mind would be useless. He had no idea when the Unidans might be able to return because he did not know what Brasald would do upon finding the Dome locked and inaccessible.

Most of the Undian camp had packed, loaded and left the day before, traveling slightly northwest to avoid going past the mountain. The scouts knew that a large river ran north to south some distance from the mountain. They would cross the river north of the mountain and then turn back south after the crossing. Vandlyn, Damond and a few others from the camp would catch up with the travelers before they crossed the river. Following their trail would not be difficult.

"Father, I'm ready." Damond said as he looked around at the empty tent. "Sad, excited, and ready," Folding the tent and adding it to their packs was all that remained to be done. Eliot and Amaz had gone on ahead as had Marna and Serad with their family. Damond smiled in spite of his sadness as he remembered Eliot strutting confidently ahead of the children herding the goats and pigs as if he were their leader. Always up for an adventure, Eliot had helped with preparations anywhere and everywhere. His joy of living made it easier for everyone around him to get through a very difficult time. "It will be

The Genesis of Atron

good to rejoin Mother and Eliot tonight, and the others," Damond mused aloud, thinking also of Marna.

"That it will, My Son. An adventure is before us, but difficulties as well. We'll be traveling through forests that haven't been explored before. We'll have to decide where to settle down again. We won't have the Dome to help us after some of our supplies run out."

"I'm so glad we can take some of the Readers with us. I don't know what we would do without The One's books. And the Readers will help us learn even more how to live from the land," Damond said. "Those years the Originals spent studying Atron, strengthening and spreading the plants and animals, will help us, won't they? And I would miss reading Jasend's diaries and the Ancients and our history."

"You're right, My Son. That will be a helpful advantage. And that will make the Readers very valuable; possessions to be cared for and guarded carefully." Vandlyn continued placing the last items into his pack.

"I hope we're not gone all that long, Father. How long do you think it will be?" Damond asked as he too stuffed items into his pack. "I don't see how we can return as long as Brasald won't follow the One?"

"It's my hope, Damond, that when Brasald can no longer use the Dome that he'll see that it's better to reunite our peoples and follow The One together. The Dome is there to help us, not to use for gain and bring us to leave the Covenant."

"How long can the Dome function without maintenance, Father?" Damond asked with concern showing in his question.

The Genesis of Atron

"It's mostly self-sufficient as you know. It seems certain to me that it could go many generations. I hope that doesn't have to be what happens though. I hope we can return and reunite with the Toldens long before then."

Vandlyn turned to pick up the finished map, checking the details once more. As he was about to place the parchment into his pack, Brasald burst through the entrance of the tent with his Tazor drawn, screaming at Vandlyn, "You locked the Dome from me! How dare you? Where is the new key?"

Staying calm, Vandlyn replied softly, "The key is hidden and will stay hidden, Brasald. You will not find it. If you stay here with your plans to be on your own, it will be without the Dome."

"Is that the map to it there in your hand? Give it to me now!" Brasald demanded.

"No, Brasald. I will not give you anything! The rest of us are leaving. Damond, put this in the pack."

As Damond took the parchment from his father's hand, Brasald's rage erupted and he fired his Tazor twice, right at Vandlyn's chest.

The shots were deadly--Vandlyn slumped to the floor.

"Nooo! Father!" Holding the parchment in one hand and reaching for his Sedat with the other, Damond waited to see what Brasald would do. It was all he could do not to go to his father and touch him.

"Give it to me, Boy." Brasald lowered his Tazor. "I don't want to hurt a boy. Put down the Sedat and hand me the map."

Braslad inched closer to Damond with his hand outstretched. "Now! Give it to me now or I will take it!"

2009 Barbara Moon

The Genesis of Atron

As Brasald grabbed the parchment, Damond kicked him in the knee and swiped at his shoulder with the Sedat. Brasald fell to the floor of the tent, bleeding from his shoulder wound, dropping his Tazor. Each had a strong hold on part of the parchment. Damond refused to let go and as Brasald fell, the parchment tore along the seams that Amaz had stitched together, leaving only half in Damond's hand. Damond grabbed the Tazor from the floor, picked up his pack and Vandlyn's Tazor and ran as fast as he could out of the tent.

I must get as far away as I can, he thought as he ran. *I must protect the parchment. The pain must wait. O, One, where are you? I can't even think. Father is dead. This can't be happening.* Damond ran and ran and ran. Following the trail left by the others, he did not stop until he could go no longer. He could not get the image out of his mind of his father lying there in the tent, dead from Brasald's hand.

Exhausted, Damond fell to the ground beside a large tree and buried his face in his hands and cried. He lay in the dirt hardly able to breathe and turned to The One Within. There was nothing he could do to change what had happened, he could only cry, bearing his pain with The One.

* * * * * *

Back in the empty Undian camp, the five others that were waiting to leave with Vandlyn heard the yelling and came to the tent in time to see Damond run off into the forest along the trail left by the Unidan travelers. Brasald was leaving the tent as they approached the entrance. He brusquely pushed them aside and limped towards the Tolden camp, holding his bleeding arm. The parchment half was not in sight but was well hidden beneath Brasald's shirt.

Entering the tent, the other Undians found Vandlyn lying there with deep burn marks on his chest. One look told them they were too late; their beloved leader was with The One. They looked at each other with deep sadness and questions in their eyes--What had happened? And why did Damond run off instead of coming to them for help?

"Who did this?" one of them demanded, looking down at his fallen friend, his sadness replaced with anger. "What is going on? Brasald has something to do with this, I'm sure."

"We'll have to sort it out later," Henric said softly as he bent over the body of his friend, "after we hear from Damond. For now we must take care of Vandlyn quickly so we can catch up with the others. We need to be with Amaz and the rest of the camp."

"I agree that we should try to rejoin them as soon as we can behind Damond," said Henric's Companion Janed. "It's going to be very painful for him to explain what happened and have to bring this terrible news to his mother and Eliot."

"What do you others say?" Henric asked, looking at them for a consensus. The others nodded.

"Then let's do what we have to do and do it quickly," Henric said as he looked around for something to wrap around his dear friend.

It was very difficult for Henric and the others to make a place to leave their friend and leader behind, especially without any time of remembrance and words about his life. They made the grave and left their friend's body with The One, knowing that Vandllyn was already there. Quickly folding Vandlyn's tent and taking his pack, they set off to follow Damond and the rest of the camp, each speaking to The One Within as they thought about how hard it was going to be for all of them to process Vandlyn's death. Never in the seasons of Atron had such a thing happened. It would be best to process it together.

The Genesis of Atron

* * * * * *

Brasald entered his tent and fell onto the cushions. The tent was filthy with unwashed plates, dirty cooking utensils and garbage. Oland was sleeping on the far side, oblivious to the events that had just taken place.

"Oland! Wake up!" his father demanded loudly. "Get me some water!"

"What?" Oland muttered as he roused from his nap. "What is it?"

"Get me some water right now. Can you not see I'm wounded? I must clean this and then decide what I'm going to do next. Go! Now!"

Oland saw the blood on his father's shoulder and jumped to his feet to do as ordered. Returning with a hide full of water, he placed it by his father's side. "What's that?" he asked, looking at the parchment with odd writing on it as Brasald drew it from his shirt and laid it on the floor? There were undecipherable markings of various colors, looking much like a young one's scribbling.

"That, you idiot, is part of a map that I must have in order to complete my plans. Here help me get this shirt off." Oland knelt down and helped his father remove his shirt. Brasald dipped a cloth into the water and began to clean his wound.

"What do we need with a map and where's the rest of it?" Oland questioned as he reached out to pick it up. "What do the markings mean?"

"I have no idea. That boy Damond has the other half. He ran off— following the rest of the Unidans out into the forest." Braslad continued to sponge his shoulder, not bothering to tell Oland the rest of the story.

The Genesis of Atron

"So why do we need this map?" asked Oland. He ran his fingers over the colors but could not figure out what any of it meant.

"Vandlyn made a new lock and key to the Dome. I can't get in there without it. This is half of the parchment map that would tell me where he hid the key. Without it, the Dome is useless."

Jumping to his feet, Oland promised, "I'll get it back for you, Father. I'll leave as soon as I get a pack together. I'll follow their trail and get it back for you."

"I'm going with you and I think we can get a few of the men to go with us. I won't be able to do much with this wound, but with all of us, we can overtake them and get the parchment back. Be ready in about fifteen minutes. Go tell the other men."

"I'll be ready," Oland said, anticipating another chance to get on his father's good side. He left quickly to find some other people to help them go after the map.

Brasald clumsily bandaged his shoulder, muttering under his breath.

* * * * * *

Damond wiped his face and got to his feet, beginning to jog, determined to push on until he caught up with the first party of travelers. With all the animals, sleds and young ones, he felt sure that they would travel slowly enough that he could catch them. He was carrying his pack with his father's and Brasald's Tazors bound to the outside; his own Tazor in its sheath at his side, the Sedat back in his belt. Damond had nowhere to put in his mind that he had actually sliced a man's skin with his Sedat, much less that he had watched while that man shot his Father with a Tazor. It was beyond his ability to figure out. There was no recourse except to turn to The One. *One, I cannot imagine life without Father. I cannot imagine how Mother will feel when she knows. This hurts so much. And Eliot. Will it take the fun and adventure from his life? How will we go on?*

Damond put one foot in front of the other, the pack weighing heavily on his back, the Tazors bumping his legs with each step. The sun was setting in front of him as he jogged west towards the big river. The shadows in the trees grew darker. He had to find where the others were camped before dark or he would have to stop. Deep in pain over the loss of his Father, he almost missed the quiet whisper in his heart. He slowed his pace to listen within. '*I am here, Damond. I have not left you. I will never leave you nor forsake you no matter what. You will go on in My strength. You will lead your people and as they follow Me, when the time is complete, they will return to the Dome. Finding your way through this loss will not be easy, but I will be with you. . .*'

The tears flowed again, almost blinding Damond as he followed the trail made by his people. *I will cling to you, O One, whenever I am afraid, whenever I feel that it's too much, too big. Thank you. Hold me and comfort me inside. I have to keep going.*

As he communed with The One, Damond wiped his tears on his shirt sleeve and kept walking. He came up over a little rise in the land and stopped. He smelled smoke. Wood smoke mixed with cooking meat. There, up ahead on the next rise he could make out the tendrils rising to the sky. He broke into a run, exhaustion forgotten, down into a dip and back up again. And now he could see the flickering light of the campfires, just a pin prick through the trees. *Thank you, Faithful One. Thank you. I've found them before dark is completely upon me.* The faster he ran the closer he came. Soon his efforts brought him close enough to call out, "It's Damond. It's Damond. I'm here."

* * * * * *

The Genesis of Atron

Henric, Janed and the rest of the party following Damond had stopped to sleep beside a clear creek that crossed the trail. They were not too far behind him, but dark had overtaken them. They ate some dried meat, some cheese and some cakes before bedding down in their cloaks. They did not even take time to put up one of the tents they were carrying. There was talk among them before going to sleep, but with the rawness of the past events, each one was content to wait until they could hear the whole story from Damond while being together with all the people. In silent agreement, they slept.

They rose with the sun and ate something from their packs, then refilling their water hides, the group set out at a fast pace hoping to find the others before they broke camp. "I have a feeling they won't hurry," Janed said to Henric interrupting his thoughts as they walked briskly, "maybe not even move at all today." She knew what he was thinking. The shock would be overwhelming.

"I feel certain you're right," Henric replied. "But I believe Brasald will follow us if he wants something badly enough to kill for it." The five kept up a steady pace hoping to find the camp before the next meal.

As the sun moved slowly across the sky, they came to the rise where Damond had stood the evening before. Still visible just a ways ahead was the smoke from the morning fires. "There they are," cried Janed with anticipation and sorrow at the same time. They all broke into a run, eating up the remaining distance with their steps.

As they neared the camp, Henric yelled as had Damond, "It's Henric. And the others."

The five cleared the trees to find the camp beside a small, bubbling stream. Several tents were set up in a circle, each facing a fire pit. The animals were tethered or corralled off to the side. The younger

The Genesis of Atron

children were down by the stream splashing and throwing stones, overlooked by one of the elders. Henric immediately saw Amaz, Eliot and Damond sitting near one of the larger fire pits surrounded by their people. He could see the pain etched on every face as they questioned again what had happened back at the old camp, waiting for these, the rest of their group to join them.

Amaz stood to receive the others. Janed embraced her, holding her tightly. "I'm so sorry, Amaz," she said with tears in her eyes. "I'm so sorry and sad with you."

Everyone stood to greet Henric and the other three with hugs and tears. Conrand hugged Henric and pulled him aside, telling him that Damond had come in alone the night before just after they'd made camp. Through his tears he had told Amaz and Eliot, in the presence of the elders and older children, what had happened to his father. "We finished our meal and just kept sitting here," Conrand said. "Most everyone is in shock and there was little sleep. We've been speaking aloud to The One, speaking to each other and simply resting here in no hurry to move on."

"We need to talk about that," Henric replied. "I don't know the whole story because Damond ran off before we knew exactly what happened. What I do know is not good. And I suspect that Brasald might be involved. He was leaving Vandlyn's tent when we got there and found Vandlyn. I fear he will follow us."

"Damond verifies that Brasald tazored Vandlyn-- trying to get the parchment map that leads to the new electrokey for the Dome. Vandlyn and Damond hid the key while we were preparing to move. Damond ran because the map ripped and he has half of it. Vandlyn had told him that Brasald must never know where the key is as long as he is set on using the Dome against the Covenant."

The Genesis of Atron

Conrand looked at Henric. They were thinking the same thing.

"That makes me feel certain now that Brasald will come after it," Henric said. "If he would kill, then he'll do whatever is necessary to get it back."

"It seems that we must help Damond for now, until some time goes by for him to grieve. As Vandlyn's oldest child, he's been training to someday have the honor and responsibility of being our leader, but he's young yet; hasn't even had his Becoming Day."

Henric nodded in agreement. "I'll speak with Damond. He'll be relieved that we're going to help him."

"After we go over the story again with you five here, if it suits you, I'll call a council to decide if we need to move on or stand against some kind of attack."

Henric nodded again.

Conrand turned to the people gathered around the fire.

"Come, let us sit again and hear all that Henric and his party know to add to Damond's story. And they need to hear Damond's story as well."

The people took their places again with Janed sitting next to Amaz holding her hand. Deblan sat at her other side. This was the way of the Unidan people—to bring what comfort they could when someone was in pain. It was enough just to sit quietly together with no need for lots of words.

Damond sat by Eliot, with Marna and Serad nearby. Their faces were puffy and and their eyes blurry from crying, their hands resting quietly in their laps. Damond told the story again of how Brasald had

The Genesis of Atron

run into their tent screaming and demanding the electrokey, how Vandlyn had been killed.

"The best thing I could think of to do," Damond said sadly, "was to run away. I had to keep Brasald from getting the parchment half. I ran and ran. The pain of what had happened was unbearable—but The One comforted me. He assured me that He was in control and confirmed to me that He would lead Unidan through me--and take the people back to the Dome in His time."

Everyone sat quietly as Damond finished. It was yet too much to take in.

Henric, Janed and the other three listened intently in order to fill in the details they had missed, aching for Damond as he spoke. Then they told everyone what they had found and how they'd made a resting place for Vandlyn before they left, hurrying to catch up with the whole camp. The time together was a time for sorrow as they all felt the pain of losing Vandlyn. They knew that as soon as they could, they would have the time for remembrance and share the words of Vandlyn's life, but for now, they would feel their sadness and sorrow.

* * * * * *

Henric, Janed, Conrand, and Deblan called a council as soon as the noon meal was finished, including the four young people in the gathering. They convened again by the fire which now blazed and crackled. The weather was moving towards the cooler season with less heat from the sun. Conrand began by speaking to The One for guidance and wisdom. "We need You and acknowledge that without You and Your direction we will not know what's best to do. Thank you, One, for your direction, as we consider our next step here after this tragedy to our people." Conrad looked around at the council, drawing strength from his friends and family. He spoke.

The Genesis of Atron

"Henric and I felt that it would be good to discuss what Brasald might do next. If he can kill to get the key and map, then most likely he will come after it. We think it best for some of us to remain here and take some kind of stand against Brasald."

Henric continued as Conrand paused, glancing around the circle noting impressions and nods of agreement. "We would send the majority of the people on ahead as soon as we finish this council, since the animals, sleds and young ones make the progress slow. We already have others packing and getting ready to leave. Those of us here, except for the young people, will stay and either stop or delay Brasald's plans. He must not have the parchment. It seems necessary to end it here; our trail is very easy to follow." Some glanced over at the other Unidans packing and loading. The young ones had grown quiet, no longer playing. They, too, were solemnly helping.

"It's very serious to think we're planning an attack or a defense," Janed added with a catch in her voice. "There is just nowhere to put this." Everyone murmured their agreement, once again feeling the sadness and abrupt changes that had come over their hearts. "Let's speak to The One again," she said.

Everyone sat quietly before The One. A few spoke aloud. Sadness and fear were present but did not prevail. Deblan raised her head and said firmly, "We must do what we have to do. We have all the people to think about. The One will bring us through it."

"Then we're in agreement?" Conrand asked. As he perceived the consensus among the group, they began to make their plans practical.

The people would leave immediately, traveling on towards the big river. Damond would lead them, along with Amaz. They would have to travel as fast as possible, to get as far away as they could. The ones remaining would rotate during the night and be on the lookout for anyone else approaching the camp. At any sign of an attack, the call would sound and all with Tazors would stand together to keep Brasald and anyone with him from taking the camp or following the rest of the people. After that, only The One knew. But they would trust Him to bring about His plan.

"Could I stay behind with you?" Eliot asked Conrand. "I can use my Tazor well. It would mean much to me if I could stay."

"And I," said Marna, looking at the elders with determination in her eyes. "Everything has changed. Please, let us help."

The elders looked at each other, holding their collective breaths. Yes, they knew the heart of a youth—that longing for adventure and that zeal to feel that their contributions matter. These two had some years before their Becoming Day, but they were right—everything had changed. Peace no longer reigned within their land. Brasald had killed; he'd left The One's ways and broken the Covenant.

This was more than an adventure, but the courage of youth was not to be taken lightly. Nor was it to be taken lightly that they were capable of contributing. Henric spoke for them all, "If your parents agree, it shall be so," he said quietly. "We hear you, though the thought of losing anymore of our people is unbearable, we hear you. You are in the hands of The One."

"I understand that I have to go," Damond added as he looked his brother in the eye. And Marna--it was hard to look at her. He did not think he could bear for her to get hurt. "I know I have to go with Mother and get the others to safety. You know I would rather stay here with you. But eventually I will take Father's place and this is part of it-- that I have to do what's best for our people."

Eliot hugged his brother tightly. What if they never saw each other again? Marna met his eyes and smiled shyly as Damond continued. "Thank you, Conrand and Henric, for taking the lead here and helping me. We'll hold you all before The One as we go." Looking around, he said quietly, "I think we should go now."

When Damond stood to go, everyone else followed. Conrand and Deblan moved to embrace their daughter then nodded and touched her Tazor sheathed at her side. Damond waited to give Marna a hug, holding her, not wanting to let go. He drew back and looked deeply into her eyes without speaking, then turned to go to his mother; Eliot followed to ask if he could stay.

* * * * * * *

Amaz's heart was torn in two. Vandlyn was gone to The One. Now Eliot wanted to stay to do battle.

Unheard of.

Unimagined.

Unknown.

How could she even take the chance of losing him, too? She spoke to The One and waited as she looked into the face of her second born. She knew the daring, carefree adventurer was yet there somewhere, but he was hidden for now behind eyes that were older and determined. She could see it. It was one of the many changes. She had to let him go—not alone—but with The One. Though her heart was pounding with feelings of the unknown before them all, she hugged her son and gave her permission. "I love you, Eliot. I will see you soon. May The One have His way." As he returned the blessing and

The Genesis of Atron

turned to rejoin the elders and scouts, Amaz felt tears run down her cheeks—the tears of a mother who knows she has to let go.

Amaz calmed her heart, wiped her tears and joined Damond at the front of the assembled travelers. Giving his first direction as their leader, he said loudly enough for all to hear, "It's time." The people began to fall into lines, their belongings secured to the sleds and wagons, the animals ready. The crowd, full of purpose, was solemn and quiet as the line began to move out.

* * * * * *

Brasald, Oland and the few who were willing to come with them approached the area of the forest around the Undian camp. It was early morning, barely light. They had eaten a cold meal and drunk some water and were creeping towards the fires they saw flickering through the trees. They were counting on surprise, expecting the Unidans would have no ideas about how to defend themselves. There was no precedent on Atron for the last several days.

Oland was beside himself with importance and anticipation. He would show his father how well he could use his Tazor and surely earn some praise when they found the parchment half and took it from Damond.

High above the ground, in the trees over the deserted camp, Conrand was keeping watch. He had already seen the Toldens sneaking through the forest. The birds had ceased chattering as they moved forward. He was waiting for just the right moment to sound the call for the others to blast their Tazors. If their plan worked they would only wound the Toldens and hopefully that was all that would happen; wound them enough that they couldn't follow and they would just give up and go back to their camp.

The Genesis of Atron

Oland was creeping ahead of his father, anxious to get the fight going. He would be the one to demand the map from Damond or whoever was hiding it. He would hold his Tazor to Damond's chest as he had with Serad that day. It had been so easy to take them to the cave. And he had not even had any punishment for it.

With Brasald and the others right behind him, Oland burst into the camp ready to fire. He stumbled in shock as he looked around. The camp was empty! Nothing but fire pits lit here and there. A few tents and the fire pits. Just as he was going to speak to his father, from high above his head, Oland heard a yell.

"Now!" cried Conrand-- and the Unidan Tazors fired. Every Tolden was instantly stunned and taken down, including Brasald and Oland. Screams of agony pierced the morning air as every one of them felt the burn of the Tazor somewhere on their body. The Unidans rushed out from around the camp and kicked the Tazors away from each Tolden, subduing them all at once. They were quickly bound with hide and tied together.

"We are sparing your lives only because of The One," Conrand growled at the prisoners. "And you, Brasald! You are blessed that we do not kill you for what you did to Vandlyn. That's what you deserve. But we'll leave you for The One as well. And if you follow us again to do harm, next time we will not be so kind."

"I will build my city without you," replied Brasald spitefully. "I don't need your parchment for now. I have my formula. That will be the beginning. And I will find a way to get into the Dome."

Looking down in disgust at this man who had caused so much pain, Conrand warned, "We're leaving now to join the rest of our people. You'll manage to get loose sooner or later. Do not follow us. We will be watching from now on."

Conrand motioned to Eliot to collect most of their Tazors, leaving a few for hunting food. Henric and Janed folded the remaining tents. Deblan and Marna doused the fires and threw all of the Toldens' food into the stream. That would make it impossible for them to follow after they got loose from their bonds. Pausing to give thanks to The One that no one was hurt, the Unidans, gathered their packs and turned to follow the path of their people.

As they watched the Unidans depart, Brasald spit his fury at his son, "This is all your fault, you idiot! You can't do anything right! I should never have let you come with me."

Oland remained quiet. It was going to be a long night before they got loose from their bonds and returned to Tolden. He would serve himself well to stay out of his father's way and not speak. The lessons were beginning to sink in: he would never be able to earn his father's acceptance no matter how hard he tried.

As the Toldens squirmed to free themselves from their bonds, rain began to fall, wetting the hides and tightening the knots. Loud, obnoxious grumbling and complaining filled the air.

CHAPTER NINE

The Unidans had been camped by the big river for several days, pitching most of the tents and planning to stay a while. Near her tent, Amaz was grinding some grain beside a small fire pit, glancing now and then at Damond as he read a stone's throw away by the river. It was so good to see him doing something that he'd always loved, moving back into a bit of normalcy.

The Genesis of Atron

After Conrand and the others had rejoined them by the river, there had been a time of thanksgiving to The One. They told the story of the ambush on Brasald and his people, relating the message given to Brasald to leave them alone. With some assurance they would not be followed, and with alert lookouts in the forest, everyone felt able to enjoy some much-needed rest.

And Amaz was very relieved and grateful that Eliot was safe after staying behind to help Conrand and the others. The seriousness of these last weeks had slightly dimmed his excitement for adventure, but she was certain that his youthful exuberance would once more show itself. For now the growing pains were strong, but he was handling them well, as were all the young people. The One was proving their commitment to Him, cementing the training they had from their parents and the elders.

And Damond--his heart was for his people, the Covenant and The One. Vandlyn would be proud of both of his sons. Amaz turned back to the grain she'd been grinding, took some in her hand and sprinkled it with water, forming some cakes. She placed more small sticks on the fire and laid the cakes in her pan, smiling at Damond when he looked up from his Reader.

Damond grinned back at his mother over by the fire pit as he thought about how comforting it was to do something as familiar as reading Jasend's diary while he sat quietly beside the water. These last weeks had been very hard, and it felt good to just sit and listen to the sounds of the camp around him. He could hear the clang of pans as they were placed on stones around the fire pits, the noisy animals as they begged to be fed or milked and the voices of his people as they worked together to carry on in spite of their pain. The people were not ready to settle down yet, but when they had finally reached the river, a modified form of their daily life had begun to reemerge, with scouts and guards now watching the surrounding forest. Soon they would pack again, cross the river and move through the forest until they found the best place to settle, but for now Damond was glad to see the children playing and people going about their evening chores.

Damond continued to read.

EARTHDATE July 2281

We've been on Atron for a year now. Father and the others think that the time has come that we can move out of the Dome. The MagnaRay produced rains that have purified the water and the air and gave great growth to the plants that were here. There were some small primitive species and insects here that adapted to the changes, and the seeds we dispersed have taken well to the new environment. It appears that all is well, the water and air perfect. I can't wait to move out. We've been able to go out some for short periods without our suits as things improved. But to live outside again! That will be the greatest.

A few weeks ago, they let the birds loose and turned out some of the pigs and all of the bearcats. We'll hunt the bearcats and the wild pigs when they grow bigger and multiply. There were some other species that were brought as frozen eggs and these have been matured and are ready to spread into the forests. I bet the goats and chickens will be glad to stay outside. I know the rest of us will be glad they have more room of their own. The Dome makes good air, but that's a lot to overcome. Phew.

There's not much left of the ship we came in. Most of it was designed for use in making the Dome and its contents. Colonists ruled by the Electorate would have ships coming and going from Earth and would not need a ship. In addition to the regular supplies, we brought

The One's books and other things that are not usually part of a new colony's supplies. Father has kept a paper log and one in a Reader of all we've done since we left. Nik and I wrote parts of it. And I've made my own log here. I wonder who will read it someday. Will it be someone like me? Someone my age? One of my descendants? Maybe reading my story will help him somehow. I hope so.

It wasn't too bad living in the Dome this year. It was a great place to play hide and seek—lots of sections and good hiding places. They let us run all over. The Instameals were good, too. Almost as good as what we had on Earth. We had lots to study and research in order to prepare for living off the land. Father and Mother say it will be different, but good. We've had to do more work already than when we lived on Earth. When we move out, Nik and I will get to explore and hunt with no fear. That will be so awesome to roam free. They hope that the fish eggs that were preserved will hatch out in the large river we saw before we landed. They already dumped the live fish that we brought. Our fathers say that Nik and I can go on the journey to the river to seed it with the remaining eggs. Again, I can't wait. And after we live outside we'll learn to use the Tazors. One of the men designed a knife for all of us to carry. It's called a Sedat and can be carried in one's belt or boot. We can use them for making things and hunting and cooking.

The other thing I can't wait to do is to go to the mountain. Father and some of the men checked it out several times over the year. They said it was like nothing they'd ever seen. It has to be from The One because the MagnaRay didn't make it. The top of the mountain is flat with a huge, deep pond there. The water turns colors at certain times and there are beautiful plants in the water. And now Father says that the water is pure enough to drink and swim in. Even though it's fairly deep, we can't really swim very well in the stream here by the Dome; it moves fast and is full of big rocks. But Father says we can swim in the mountain pond, or when we go to the big river if there has not been too much rain. Nik and I can't wait to do that once again.

Damond ran his fingers through his hair and stretched as he looked up from Jasend's diary. It truly was good to do something that he'd done before they left the Dome. These days the people had spent beside the big river had been healing for everyone. Just a bit of the edge had been taken from the pain, but Damond knew life would never be exactly the same. Most of all Damond knew nothing could ever take the place of his father. He would have to cling to The One to bear it. But Eliot and Marna, and the others, were safe. He was grateful to The One that all had gone well when confronting Brasald and they hoped that Brasald would not follow them. He could focus on these positives in spite of his loss.

Although he felt sad about so many changes, Damond drew some comfort from reading how eager Jasend was to explore his new home. *My people are on the brink of exploring, too,* he thought as he looked at the big river, wide and rushing by. *We're all safe, we've had time to rest and now the scouts are making plans for how to cross the river. There is much to do.* Damond sighed, relaxing his shoulders, reminding himself to put his burdens on The One. *Now I certainly understand better how Jasend felt leaving everything and starting over.* Damond smiled at the thought of all he'd read about Jasend. *Adventures are exciting and difficult at the same time, just like Jasend said. But like him, I have my family, my friends and The One.*

As they so often did, Damond's thoughts turned again to his father and how much he missed him. He thought about how much he would have to learn in order to become the leader he knew his father would want him to be. But he took strength from Jasend's words and reminded himself, *I have many to help me. And The One is my life, my constant source. Mother is here, always here. I see how she goes on through her pain.* He looked over at her again, smiling when their eyes met.

And Eliot, he thought. *I have Eliot, too. I see he's changed, but it isn't bad, just different.* Damond took a moment to think about that. *I wonder if I've changed, too--and how. I suppose I have; we all have. Marna, too.*

Thinking of Marna always warmed his heart and made it thump a little faster. *She's more than a friend.* He smiled again, stilling his heart. *But it isn't time. I haven't even chosen my First Companion yet, much less to be thinking of my Last.*

As he moved around to get more comfortable, his thoughts about First and Last Companions took him on another path. *Maybe we'll have to change the age for our Becoming Days now. We've all had to grow up quickly.*

He glanced again at his mother, watching her work on the fire, preparing their meal. The younger boys had figured out how to catch the fish they saw in the river. After a few experiments on how to clean and prepare them, everyone had been enjoying a change of diet.

Damond continued to ponder Becoming Days and Companions: *Eliot would be my choice for First Companion. I know it doesn't have to be a brother or sister, but he would be my choice. I'll talk to Henric and Conrand about it. Changing the age will make some other scary and exciting adventures to think about.*

Closing the Reader, Damond went to put it in his pack. "Mother, do you need some more water?" he asked. Eliot and several of the young children were throwing rocks into the river downstream from where Damond had been reading. It was good to hear them laughing.

"That would be helpful, Son," said Amaz. The days were yet warm enough that she was cooking outside most of the time. "Here's a hide you can use. I'll need more after we eat, but one will do for now. Thank you."

"I'll help you when I get back," said Damond as he took the hide bucket from his mother. Walking back down the small hill towards the water, he called to Eliot, "Hey, Eliot, where are the girls?"

"They're in their tent helping their mother."

"See if they want to do some Tazor practice after the meal. I'm feeling a little out of practice."

Eliot skipped his last stone across the water, telling the children thanks for playing with him and walked back up the hill over to the girls' tent. "Marna, Serad! You want to do some Tazor practice after the meal? Damond's says he's out of practice. Maybe we can beat his shot."

It was so good to hear the lilt of teasing back in Eliot's voice. "Surely," Serad answered as she came out the tent entrance. "I'll take up that challenge." She smiled at Eliot.

"I, too," Marna interjected, sticking her head out the door. It felt good to smile and think about enjoying some practice like they'd done before. "Maybe we can all three beat him this time."

"Are you up to it, Dame? Us beating you and all?" teased Eliot as Damond sat down to help Amaz finish cooking.

Damond grinned. "We shall see," was his only answer. "See you after the meal."

CHAPTER TEN

Oland was alone in the forest. The birds were singing, the sun just above the eastern horizon. Since their failure to retrieve the parchment, he had stayed away from his father and their camp even more than usual. It wasn't worth it to hear his father's remarks and feel the sting of his anger and disgust. Sometimes Oland took a tent, his Tazor and some food and camped for a while by himself, always being wary of the huge vines. He'd seen evidence of some other huge plants growing out of control and had been careful to skirt them with plenty of room to spare. *Does Father even know what's going on with these plants?* he wondered to himself as he stooped to drink from the stream near his current camp. *I'm certainly not going to tell him. He can find out for himself-- maybe the hard way. Best to stay clear of him <u>and</u> the plants.* Water dripping from his face, Oland sat back on his heels at the edge of the stream. Suddenly, a loud crash coming from the bushes behind him made him jump, nearly causing him to tumble into the water. *What was that?*

"Who's there," he demanded aloud. No one answered. He heard the crash again. It sounded like small trees falling over. He stood up and turned in a circle checking every direction. *Was it possible one of those vines could make a noise as it was growing?* He was frozen with fear, afraid to move from the spot where he was standing. He'd never heard a sound that loud.

CRASH! The noise was louder and closer. Finally Oland's fear thawed enough for him to scuttle behind a large rock right upstream.

CRASH!

Again. And closer.

The Genesis of Atron

Now he could smell a horrible, overpowering odor that made him want to throw up. Something flattened a small bush near the edge of the trees. At the next crash, a large leg came into view followed by an even larger furry, brown body and three other legs. Attached to the body, towering almost as high as some of the small trees was a round head with a pointed snout, mouth open and growling, showing sharp, yellow teeth. The creature headed for the stream, burying its face in the water, lapping noisily. The creature was like nothing Oland had ever seen before.

His whole body shaking, his teeth chattering, Oland dared to watch the creature from behind the rock. *It looks like a bearcat,* he thought. *But what's happened to it? I've never seen one that huge.*

After drinking its fill, the ugly creature turned and lumbered off back into the forest, flattening more large bushes and knocking down small trees as it went, filling the air with its stench. Oland waited until it was quiet again, quickly broke camp, and fled back towards the Tolden camp to tell his father what he had seen. This had to be connected to the experiments that Brasald had been doing with his spray formula. It was apparently affecting more than just plants. Oland had no idea what they could do about it or whether his father could reverse any of it. All he knew for now was that he did not want to see anymore huge vines or furry brown bearcats more than ten times their normal size.

* * * * * *

Oland found his father close to the Dome, walking around it as if in a daze. Brasald stopped long enough to listen to Oland's story about the huge creature he'd seen in the forest, not really caring one way or the other. "Leave me, Oland. I have important work to do and you're in my way." Oland was not surprised at his father's reaction. When had he ever listened to anything he had to say?

Brasald continued his verbal assault as he walked away. "I have many more experiments in my plan. I'll take care of the creature later. Now go find something to do."

Oland stood there amazed as his father began circling the Dome, touching its surface as he walked. *What is going on?* Oland wondered.

The presence of a huge creature was not nearly as important to Brasald as was his desire to get into the Dome. After their failure to retrieve the other half of the parchment, Brasald had set his mind on little else. He still had some of the orange liquid hidden inside his tent, but he wanted to work on other projects and use more of the technology from the Originals. This obsession seemed to be interfering with his thinking, sending him daily to circle the Dome looking for a way to enter it again.

* * * * * * *

Since returning from the forest and seeing his father's strange behavior at the Dome and his dismissal about the awful creature, Oland had been following his father from a distance to see what was going on. For the last few days, Oland had watched Brasald circle the Dome, knocking on it and peering closely at its solid, slick surface.

It remained impenetrable.

I think Father is losing his mind, Oland thought as he watched his father circle the Dome for the second time that morning. Oland was sitting in a clump of trees where he could see his father but not be seen. *Why doesn't he give up? Everyone knows the Dome is solid. And what is he going to do about the horrible creature I saw? Somebody needs to do something. I don't ever want to see one of those again.*

The Genesis of Atron

Oland usually kept clear of the Dome area and only his father's strange behavior had enticed him to be near it. He had tried to convince his father about the bearcat and to stop obsessing about the Dome, but Brasald refused to listen either way. Hateful remarks were all he'd received for his efforts. *Today is the last time I'm going to follow him,* Oland said to himself. *He won't listen to anything I say. Why do I even try? It's clear that he hates me.*

Brasald suddenly wandered away from the edge of the Dome towards one of the large vines. Parts of the vine were climbing a nearby tree; other parts were lying on the ground. Oland stood to leave, peering through the bushes at his father one last time.

"FATHER! NO! NO!" Oland screamed!

But it was too late. Just as Braslad stooped to look at one of the huge leaves, the giant blossom right above him dropped down and slammed itself over the top of his head, completely covering his entire body. A loud slurping sound pierced the air as the enormous bloom rose again towards the top of the trees, shuddering until it was still.

Brasald was gone.

"AYYYY!" Oland screamed again, wanting to vomit.

There was nothing he could do except run away.

PART TWO—Many Changes

CHAPTER ONE

EARTHDATE August 2448

It's been an Earth year since Father was killed, and we crossed the big river, Damond wrote, *moving through the forests as needed until we found the place where we wanted to settle. The ache is ever present without Father, but The One is faithful with His comfort. I still love to read Jasend's diary, but now I'm keeping one of my own since we're no longer at the Dome and able to make the log reports. I'm very careful with my Reader, which continues to work well, but several that we brought with us have been damaged or lost. No one knows when we'll return to the Dome so life must go on with less and less expectations of access to its marvels. The parchment is safely hidden and I guard it with my life. As we moved, I added a few notes to it, continuing to disguise them with riddles. The berry ink will not be as permanent as that from the Dome, but of course I hope that we will be able to go back before fading would be a big problem. But I take no chances that just anyone can decipher it all, even though Father and I felt that only a true follower would be able to. Now and then I do wonder if it isn't likely that I'll have to pass it down to my son or daughter for them to guard, along with the story of what happened last year. Only The One knows, so I try not to worry, trusting that He is faithful as always.*

The scouts and elders worked together to design some rafts that carried us and our possessions across the river. It was a very difficult crossing as the river runs strong and high. One of the rafts capsized, dumping everything into the water. We watched the tents and supplies being swiftly swept away, but were most thankful no lives were lost. When everyone was safe on the other side, our relief was such that we camped there for a while, renewing our strength and thanking The One. We felt a little less anxious about any Toldens that might try to attack us again, and as we'd hoped, many months passed before we heard anything from the Toldens' camp.

We finally settled in a fertile area with plenty of forests for wood to use and animals to hunt, clearing land for our grain. We chose a spot far enough away from the big river to assure that our camp and fields would be spared if the river flooded. A clear, heavily flowing stream passes right through the new camp, close enough for hauling water but not likely to flood. We sowed the grain fields between us and the big river.

One day the scouts saw two strangers approaching the area where our grain grows. They were dressed like Toldens but not recognizable from a distance. The scouts approached them cautiously with Tazors drawn. They recognized the two as coming from Brasald's camp and escorted them in to meet with the elders. Their words were that Brasald was dead and Oland was now the leader. The experiments had not gone well and some of the people wanted to rejoin the neighbors they'd grown up with. Oland was interested in an agreement to live closer together again, saying he too was ready to leave the Dome and would follow the Covenant and The One.

After a long discussion and time with The One, the elders agreed to give the Toldens another chance, as it seemed to them that would be the way of The One. Only through His strength in us had we been able to forgive all that had happened, and though we had no desire to live as close as we once had, we held no bitterness. The scouts returned to their camp and after several weeks we saw the Toldens making a new camp near our grain fields, between us and the big river. They sowed some grain of their own, but in a much smaller field than ours.

Sadly for everyone, it didn't take long to realize that Oland was like his father and nothing had changed at all. There was no evidence that he followed The One, though there were some Toldens who still wished to follow Him. Oland began to build what he planned to turn into a city some day. When asked about the decision to leave the Dome area, he would not tell the elders what had gone wrong with the experiments. He would only say that it was extremely dangerous to live close to the Dome any more, warning everyone not to go back across the big river, especially north of the camps.

Since their arrival, our peoples don't work well together as we did before and the discord is difficult. I do believe there are a few who miss the old ways, but most refuse to interact with us. Many don't follow The One and often mock us when we talk of Him. I seldom see Oland and don't wish to--he is not one whom we can trust.

Damond looked up as Eliot entered the tent where he was writing. "I'm going to the fields. Do you want me to wait for you?" Eliot asked.

"I'm almost finished with this entry. Can you wait?"

"I'll wait," Eliot replied as he turned to go back outside. "I'll check with Marna and Serad."

"That would be great," Damond said. "I won't be long." He turned back to his Reader. Hearing Marna's name quickened his pulse, but he stuck to his task.

Shortly after we crossed the river and got settled, I asked the elders about changing the age for Becoming Days. It seemed to me that we young people had grown up quickly and I thought for at least a time, we might consider doing it earlier. We could continue to study with the elders, but have the ceremonies at sixteen seasons instead of eighteen. The elders spoke with The One and soon the fifteen of us with sixteen seasons prepared for our Day. I was very sad that Father was not there. Mother said he would have been very proud. Conrand and Henric shared the words and led the ceremony while we spoke our pledges. I chose Eliot as my First Companion; Marna chose Serad. Each of us pledged as First Companions, as had our mothers and fathers before us, to speak truth which each other at all times and to practice with each other the qualities we need in order to live closely with another. Then we pledged to keep our bodies pure and sacred before The One, to be shared only with our Last Companion.

It was a sobering day for the whole camp, and very moving to go through my Becoming Day earlier than usual, bringing me a stronger sense of responsibility to honor my pledges and the elders' trust. I'm sensing The One moving me towards Marna as my Last Companion, but I know it's too soon to make that decision since most usually wait until after twenty seasons. There's plenty of time to test it and find His way for certain.

"Hey, Damond, are you coming?" Eliot stuck his head back in the tent. The girls were close behind.

"I'm finished," Damond responded as he closed his Reader and put it away. The four young people left for the fields, speaking to their families they passed who were at work, milking the goats, tending the food gardens or grinding grain.

CHAPTER TWO

EARTHDATE September 2498

The years are many since we crossed the river. So many changes. I'm growing older as are many who crossed with me. The people's memories of the Dome are not as sharp and clear as they once were. It's not there before us every day as it used to be, where we could see the MagnaRay's purple beam streak through the sky and watch the colors bounce off the top of the Dome whenever the sun struck its surface. I'm writing the log reports now on pieces of thin bark or hides as the last Reader is not working as it should. Soon I will have to resort to word of mouth only. When that day comes, there will be great sorrow and sadness that we can no longer read the books of The One. Though we teach the young ones and pass His ways on by word of mouth, not being able to read His books by oneself will be mourned by everyone.

But the parchment is safe. Just as I wondered long ago, I will be passing it down to my son, Kolen. It won't be long until I give it to him and Elezaban for safe keeping. They expect their baby soon, life continues and The One is faithful. Kolen will be a great father and as good a leader as he is a son. He's listened well and learned the ways of The One, the ways of our people.

The Genesis of Atron

Times grow harder. Since the Toldens returned with Oland as their leader, there is much unrest. Rumors are all that's left of their reasons for leaving the Dome and following us here. Because we can see the probable end of having The One's books to read, some elders have debated going back to the Dome. But the warnings we heard and the rumors that continue are very harsh against going back. Something about the plants. I remember he was trying to increase growth of the plants with his experiments. The worse rumors are that Brasald's experiments affected more than just a vine or two—maybe even some animals. The elders deemed the danger too unknown to take a risk at this time, so we will eventually lose the books. The people have taken to calling the area on the other side of the big river, "the Beyond."

Oland has not been a good leader, following The One even less than his father did. An ugly rift grows larger between our peoples where once we lived as one. I've heard that Oland is ready as I am to pass his leadership to his son. I expect it to become worse. They want to control the grain fields that lie closest to the river.

Damond paused in his writing, glancing over at his beloved Marna where she sat sewing. Their years together had been wonderful and full with The One and their families, forging a new life. Their tent was full of cushions and pillows woven and stuffed with love by hands eager to serve. The seasons had passed with their usual mildness and regular weather to assure good crops and good hunting. For Damond, this time at the end of the day's work was his favorite. As he watched Marna for a moment, his thoughts wandered back to that day when he had gone to talk to his mother about taking Marna as his Last Companion.

"Mother." Damond sat down beside Amaz as she tended the fire pit outside. "Can we talk?"

"Certainly, Son. What's in your thoughts?" Amaz broke some small sticks into small pieces and fed the fire until it was blazing and ready for some larger pieces of wood. She stirred the mixture for the flat cakes and prepared the strips of meat, placing them to sizzle on the far side of the fire.

"It's been two seasons since we crossed the river. I know it's sooner than usual, much sooner than the times I've read so much about since Jasend and his family came to Atron." Damond stumbled over his words as he fidgeted and picked up some more sticks to put into the fire.

"Go on, Dame." His mother smiled slightly as she anticipated the direction of his conversation.

"I want to take Marna as my Last Companion." There. He'd said it aloud. Not certain what response he would get, he sat looking at the fire.

"And with whom have you discussed this idea?" Amaz asked with a real smile.

"I speak with The One about it quite often," he answered looking up to see what her reactions were going to be. He saw her smile and let out a sigh, not realizing he'd been holding his breath.

"And who else?" prodded Amaz. "Have you spoken to any of the elders?"

"I did mention it to Henric once."

"And what did Henric say about it?"

"To keep speaking to The One and to talk to you."

"What about the intended Last Companion? Do you know how she feels?"

"I believe she's in agreement. It's been unspoken between us for the last few seasons. But I wanted to talk to you first and ask if you will go with me to talk to her father and mother? It is unusual to ask this soon. We only have eighteen seasons."

"Of course, My Son, you know I will. It will not be a surprise to Conrand and Deblan," Amaz said. She placed some cakes upon the fire as the meat splattered and grew crisper. "If Marna is ready, I believe we parents can give our blessing, though it's different and not as we've done in the past."

"Then I'll talk with Marna tonight before we go to their tent."

Our ceremony was simple but meaningful and I would not know what to do without her, Damond remembered. He smiled to himself as his thoughts returned to the present there in the tent at the end of the day. *And now we are soon to have another generation with Kolen's baby. How Mother would have loved this day, to see a new one come into the world. It was so extremely difficult to lose her, too. But it helps to know she's with The One face to face. . .* The pain tugged at his heart reminding him again how much they all missed her.

"Marna!" Damond's thoughts were interrupted by Serad's voice as she entered the tent. "Come! Elezaban is nearing her time. Kolen sent me for you. And I'm going for her mother as well."

Marna gathered her cloak and supplies, placed a kiss on Damond's cheek and hurried out the door after Serad. As she left she turned to smile at her Companion, the understanding of their love, plus the shared joy of a new arrival, passing between them.

CHAPTER THREE

Sandlen was bouncing with excitement, her blue eyes sparkling with joy while her bare feet stirred little tufts of dust all around. Her light brown hair, the color of her mother's, hung almost to her waist and flowed sideways and up and down as she bounced. Her pants and shirt were a smaller copy of the colorfully dyed shirts that her Unidan elders wore every day. She waited expectantly by the stream, unable to stand still thinking about how Grandfather Damond and Great Uncle Eliot were going to do her first lesson on how to use the Tazor. She'd now passed ten seasons and Father said she could begin her training. Since Grandfather and Uncle Eliot were so old, she just knew that soon, with lots of practice, she could do better than they with her Tazor. Of course she'd have to work harder to pass up her Father because he wasn't quite so old.

"Are you ready, Little One?" asked Damond as he walked up to Sandlen' watching her dance with joy. He leaned over and gave her a big hug. "Let's head for the target area."

"Oh, yes, yes! Grandfather! I've been so ready for days. I can't wait."

"Well, one thing for sure," added her uncle, "you got your love for adventure and your enthusiasm for life from your old uncle here."

"Am I really like you, Uncle Eliot?" It was obvious to all that he was one of her favorite people in the camp.

"That's for sure, Sweet Girl. And don't forget it. Come on. Let's go."

The trio headed towards the target area, an old stump much like the one Sandlen's grandparents had practiced on long ago near the Dome.

The Genesis of Atron

Today's first lesson would be about the secret of the Tazor—how to be in tune with The One in order to blast the light farther and stronger. Later Sandlen and the other children would practice sword thrusts and parries as well.

Damond delighted in watching Sandlen's eagerness to learn the ways of her people. He could see she was a true child of Unidan. It was obvious to him that Kolen and Elezaban walked with The One and loved her joyfully. He had watched them discipline her with love and patience, allowing her to learn from her mistakes without being humiliated.

Damond remembered watching Sandlen when she was younger as her mother patiently taught her to help with all the work in the camp. "I don't like to do all this work," she would protest. "I don't want to milk the goats or hoe in the garden. I don't want to be with the smelly sheep. I want to hunt for the eggs."

Damond laughed to himself as he remembered Elezaban's favorite story about Sandlen always wanting to hunt for eggs, but like her Uncle Eliot, she didn't like to carry water from the stream. Sandlen knew that old story about Uncle Eliot's challenge from Aunt Serad. They told it often and still laughed about it.

Like the other mothers in Unidan, Elezaban was seldom ever harsh with Sandlen's childish balks at the hard things they had to do. And when Elezaban was impatient or irritable, she always asked Sandlen to forgive her. Damond had personally experienced Sandlen's grasp on that lesson over the years as she learned to ask forgiveness of others whom she had offended. Now, at ten seasons, Sandlen was fairly good at doing hard things and today she would begin Tazor training. Though it was hard practice, all the children loved the Tazor lessons.

The Genesis of Atron

It warmed Damond's heart to know that after all these years since the Orginials came, the Unidans still taught their children of The One and His ways, guiding them by example and words to grow to love Him as they did. Love and acceptance permeated the Unidan camp as everyone interacted with one another through the ways of The One. When old enough to understand all that was involved in following Him, each child would receive The One within for themselves. Sandlen had already done this last season.

As if she knew he was thinking about her, Sandlen looked up at Damond and smiled. "This is a big day for me, Grandfather. I can't wait to begin."

"It is that, Sandlen. And I know you will do well." Damond returned the smile. "You have learned many hard lessons and though this one will be difficult, too, it will also be great fun."

It was good to know that Sandlen was not only learning the ways of The One and how to do hard work, but she was also learning of their ancestry and why they were on Atron. She had heard the stories of the Originals' travels from Earth and the marvels of the Dome, which was now far away and inaccessible. Although the young ones heard lots of stories, with the passing of the years since leaving the Dome and losing the Readers, some details of Atron's past were becoming dim. Damond knew that with his generation's passing, the light would most likely grow dimmer.

Over the years, Damond had watched the Toldens' way of life deteriorate greatly when it came to following The One and learning of their past. Most had ceased to follow Him years ago, not even remembering who He was; some even doubting that there was a Dome. Sandlen was not allowed to go to the Tolden city that had grown up closer to the big river. It was not safe. The old Tolden king, Oland, had died, and his son was worse than he had been. He was

The Genesis of Atron

greedy and hungry for power. Compared to the Unidans and most in his city, he lived luxuriously, taking what he wanted from his people.

Damond frowned as he thought about how close the Unidans' grain fields were to the city. Some of the Unidan elders feared that the Toldens might take over their fields. During the last few seasons, the rainfall had lessened in its cycle for some reason and some were concerned that a drought was on the way. Those who had read the Ancients' books had read of these things happening on Earth, though in their lifetimes here on Atron the rain had always fallen faithfully and regularly. Less rainfall could spell disaster for Unidan's food supply. Damond did not know exactly how the MagnaRay affected Atron's weather, but sometimes he wondered if going back to the Dome might help. But between the rumors of great danger back at the Dome that Oland's people had carried to the camps and knowing that the forests had now grown thicker, the Unidans were not willing to risk trying to find the Dome without the other half of the parchment that Damond had passed down to Kolen.

As they neared the practice stump, Sandlen put her hand into Damond's, interrupting his musings. "There it is, Grandfather," she announced with glee. "Can I hold the Tazor now? When are you going to tell me the secret?"

Damond chuckled at her eagerness as he drew his Tazor from its sheath. The blade shone in the sunshine, the handle black and strong. The row of red buttons seemed to blink at Sandlen as she reached out to touch the Tazor where her Grandfather's fingers grasped the hilt. "It won't be long, Precious One," he said.

Arriving at the stump, Eliot threw the hide he was carrying over the pock-covered stump. "This reminds me of how your grandmother Marna and your Aunt Serad used to practice Tazors with us when we were young," Eliot said to Sandlen as she watched him settle the hide. "I used to compete with your Grandfather."

"I know that story, Uncle Eliot," Sandlen said with a big grin. "I've heard it many times." Turning to Damond, she asked, "Would you tell it again, Grandfather?"

"Well, as you've heard," he began, "once Uncle Eliot thought he could beat my best shot and when he missed, he had to carry Aunt Serad's water and his own for three days." Grandfather Damond laughed heartily, slapping Eliot on the back. "We teased him for seasons." Eliot's smile made his wrinkles deepen and Sandlen looked from one to the other with delight.

"What do you mean 'seasons,' Dame?" Eliot returned. "You've never stopped."

"Well, we have to get back at you somehow," Damond retorted.

"I'm planning to beat you, Grandfather," Sandlen said confidently, rejoining the conversation. "You're old, you know."

"We shall see, Little One," Damond said, giving her another hug, this time picking her up and swinging her around before putting her down. "Now let's talk about how this Tazor works."

Sandlen listened carefully as the men showed her the various ways to use a Tazor. She was intrigued by the Unidan secret that involved focusing on The One. She determined to practice every day with anyone who would help her until she could do it herself. Like the young ones before her, Tazor practice would be the most fun part of the day. Chickens, goats, sheep and pigs needed tending. Grain had to be picked or ground and water carried. There was always work to do

The Genesis of Atron

around the camp, but Tazor practice gave everyone something fun to look forward to between the chores of work.

Practicing the Tazor was a fun path to self-discipline and Sandlen was learning it well. Sometimes she still didn't feel like helping Mother with all the work that had to be done. Sometimes she wanted more than her share of the special cakes Mother made from the berries that grew around the forest. But slowly and surely Sandlen was coming to realize that some things were satisfying, and others were not and that she could do things she didn't feel like doing. These daily lessons of life and how it works within The One's plan were preparing her to advance her knowledge and skill in living life there in Unidan as she moved closer to her Becoming Day. And some day she would be the next leader of Unidan, with children of her own.

CHAPTER FOUR

Sandlen sat by the stream outside her tent, brushing her long hair and thinking about Grandfather Damond and the others who had already gone to be with The One. Was it not just yesterday when she was teasing him about doing better than he with her Tazor? It seemed that the seasons had flown by too fast and here she was with a child of her own. Her eyes closed for a moment and she smiled as she remembered the day that she had finally conquered the secret of the Tazor and made a shot that beat her grandfather's. *I've always wondered if I really beat him or if he let me beat him,* she mused. *I could see it either way. S*he remembered with great respect how honest he was, but also how kind and loving. *I was only twelve. But he and Uncle Eliot both said I had a good touch and a good focus on The One. And I suppose that's the most important thing anyway.*

The Genesis of Atron

It was late afternoon and the shade by the water felt cool as she rested and watched Karand toddle around nearby, picking up sticks and making them into a pretend fire pit. Now and then Karand looked up at her, her blue eyes sparkling and the sun shining through her blond hair. Sandlen put down her brush. It was almost time to milk the goats.

The years had brought many changes. Grandfather Damond had changed the Becoming Day back to eighteen seasons after the people had been settled for a while. Sandlen remembered her Becoming Day so clearly, how she and her mother had worked on her beautiful dress. It was very different from the plain pants and shirts that everyone wore for daily work. It felt so lovely to feel the flowing skirt rustle around her feet when she walked, and the stitching around the neckline was colorful and becoming to her eyes.

And then the day that Jazen and I became Last Companions and I wore my beautiful dress again, Sandlen smiled to herself, her thoughts turning to her other special day. *Grandfather was here for that and I'm glad that he was, but I wish he were here to see Karand. I know he would be proud. How he would love her as he did me, teaching her patiently all the ways of life. I want to teach her everything Grandfather taught me. . .*

Sandlen's musings were interrupted by her daughter's little hands gently touching her face.

"Look, Mama, pretty flower." Karand handed her a slightly smashed, damp pink flower that she had picked by the path.

"A most wonderful gift from my most wonderful girl," Sandlen responded with a hug that ended quickly as Karand moved off for more exploring.

I'm afraid our Unidan history is slowly getting lost, Sandlen's thoughts returned to her musings. *Without the Readers that the people used to have and no books, it's quickly becoming more difficult to keep all the stories together. I have the parchment that Grandfather saved. It's torn in half and no one knows where the other half is. Grandfather told the stories, about the old Dome, a key, an electrokey, he called it, and the parchment. He also knew stories about the Originals and why they came here. The parchment is a secret and Father has told me many times how it must be guarded closely without fail in case we find the other half and can ever return to the Dome. Too much time has passed to return without it. And everyone says it's very dangerous out there in the Beyond.*

Sandlen looked up to check on Karand who was continuing to explore around the tents, picking more flowers. *Those who come and go from the fields say that it's getting worse in the city and much more difficult to work safely in the fields. There's a lot of hatred from the Toldens, too. They don't want to share the fields and there are rumors they may take over the paths to the big river that help water the fields when the rain is scarce. Grandfather seemed to think going back to the Dome would help fix the rain problem as well, but it always seemed best to wait on a clear leading from The One.*

Sandlen rose from her place by the stream and headed for their tent to gather what she needed to milk the goats and prepare the evening meal. As she milked and kept an eye on Karand, she spoke to The One about the problems she'd been thinking about. *More changes are coming,* she sensed as her feelings stirred, bringing a tinge of dread. *How much more will go wrong? What will our children have to endure? But,* she caught herself, turning to The One, *as the Elders have taught us and we have seen for ourselves in many ways, You are with us.* 'You are our strength in time of trouble,' she said to Him, reminding herself of the Ancients' teachings.

The Genesis of Atron

Karand toddled over to pet the goat and "help" her mother. Seeing her little daughter's joy for life and talking to The One made it much easier for Sandlen to look past the worries and fears that so often wanted to intrude on her peace.

* * * * * *

Grandfather Kolen and Grandmother Elezaban sat with others around the large fire pit at the edge of the meeting square, keeping their eyes on little Karand playing in the dirt with Lornen, her favorite friend, and several other young ones. The camp had finished the evening meal and cleaned up the remains, cared for the animals and most had gathered in the square to enjoy some time together. The people who played instruments were off to one side deciding what tune to begin with.

"Don't you love this time of the evening?" Elezaban said to Kolen as she glanced around at their friends and the children playing together. The square was crowded tonight and the air was filled with talking and laughing.

"Any time there is music and dancing is a time I love to be out," answered Kolen. "Will you dance with me when they decide what to play first?"

He already knew the answer. Elezaban never turned down a chance to dance.

"And well you know that I will," she confirmed, laughing at the grin on his wrinkled face. "I'm sure if I don't, you can get Karand to twirl with you. She loves to dance as much as we do."

The musicians began to play their flutes, their drums and their stringed instruments. Most of the people got up to dance while the others kept time tapping their feet or clapping their hands. Karand, dizzy with delight, twirled gleefully around her grandparents, her hair flying free from its braid.

Those not listening or dancing to the music in the Square were resting in their tents or walking along the paths in the shade of the evening. It was good to have a more permanent camp, with its combination of tents from the Originals intermingled with tents that the people had made from hides as the camp grew over the years.

With the scouts rotating their protection, the people could enjoy their free time without fear, and the young ones could run freely throughout the camp and the surrounding forest up to the points that the scouts had marked. Outside those marks the lookouts kept a watchful eye for any threat that might arise from the Toldens.

As they went about their lives, concerns about the growing division and threats with the Toldens, and the living conditions of the people, were not far from the Unidans' thoughts. Living in the city was very different from living in their camp. The city was dirty and disorderly, rotting garbage often thrown out windows or doors into the alley ways. Shop keepers sold their wares in the streets where most people argued and sometimes fought over the wares. The children ran loose without supervision and often caused trouble throughout the city. And so unlike the Unidans, it seemed that no one there wanted to know about The One and His ways. Even as they enjoyed an evening of resting or dancing, the Unidans desired to help those with whom they were once united.

"Kolen! Kolen!"

The wavering shout interrupted the music and various conversations flowing around the large fire. Everyone turned to see who was calling. Kolen and Elezaban rose hurriedly from their places by the fire where they were resting between tunes. They saw Eliot just entering the square from the path beside the stream, the old man trying to run, but hardly able to walk from the exertion.

"What is it?" Kolen asked as he ran to meet his elderly uncle. Eliot could barely speak, his old legs wobbling, his breath coming in spurts as he tried to speak.

"Aarnon. . . just returned. . . from the fields!" Eliot panted, holding his stomach, taking deep breaths. "Some Toldens came into the fields . . . and took some of our people. He's behind me, helping some of the others. . . who tried to fight."

"You must be careful, Uncle. But we understand your concern. Get your breath."

Eliot tried again. "Serad is with them. . . We were taking a walk when we saw them limping towards us. . . I ran ahead to tell you."

As Eliot's breathing calmed, Kolen and the other elders hurried ahead of him to Aarnon's tent where his Companion and Serad were helping the wounded survivors and getting more details.

While Serad bandaged a cut on Aarnon's arm, he relayed the story. "We were gathering our tools to return for the evening when a group of Toldens burst into the field with Tazors drawn. I've never seen anyone dressed as they were. All of the men were wearing matching clothes. They demanded that we put down our Tazors and stand still."

The other worker continued, "We put down our Tazors, but not our Sedats. We tried to fight, but they took control. Then they told us— 'We are the soldiers of King Talbot, grandson of the mighty Oland. He declares that you will work these fields for the good of all. We are taking three of you with us to assure your cooperation. If you do not comply with all that our king demands, not only will you not see them again, but we will raid your camp.'"

"Elezaban," Kolen said, interrupting the story and turning to his Companion, "Please go quickly and tell the scouts to spread out into the forest towards the direction of the fields and Tolden. We must speak to The One and make some plans."

Elezaban left to deliver the instructions to the scouts and they rushed to the forest to double their lookouts around the camp. She then went to find Sandlen and Jazen who had come from their tent when they heard the shouting. She quickly related Aarnon's story and added, "Come with me, please. I'm going to tell the people what's going on. You two will need to join the council after everyone goes back to their tents. We have to make some plans."

Sandlen and Jazen looked at each other as they walked towards the square. It was almost too much to take in; it was happening so fast. They gathered the people and helped quiet the young ones as Elezaban stood on a log in order to be heard well. She quickly told the people about the report from Aarnon and asked everyone except the leaders to go back to their tents and stay there until morning. She knew that each family would speak to The One and offer comfort for those whose family members had been taken.

As the people dispersed, taking the young ones with them that needed care, Kolen approached the square to join the council who would make plans and divide up the necessary tasks to defend the camp. He gestured for them to sit. "This report is serious. We have no idea where the soldiers took our people, nor will it be easy to find out. This changes everything."

Kolen paused as if to allow the news to sink in to everyone's mind, including his own. "New plans must be made to defend ourselves, and to find a way to discover where the others are being kept inside Tolden."

"I'll make some other weapons to supplement our Tazors and Sedats," offered Ryese, Jazen's friend and father of Lornen.

"That would be very helpful," Kolen replied. "Thank you, Ryese. Let's go to The One and see what He says." The group sat quietly speaking to The One Within. After a short time, Kolen spoke to Him aloud and then they discussed their impressions.

"We need to have a plan for defense should the Toldens take action on their threat to make a raid," said Sandlen. "I think it would be wise to have a set boundary in the eastern forest to divide our camp from their area and to make sure none of the young ones can go past that edge."

"Good idea, Daughter," Kolen said, looking around and seeing nods of agreement. "What else?'

"This is going to be very difficult for all of us at first," interjected Jazen. "It's so much a part of our life not to fight and not to hate. Only The One can direct us."

"That's true," Eliot agreed. "For generations we've trained and practiced with our Tazors, but never to hurt another person. The need to defend our camp calls for drastic changes. Only with The One's strength in us will be able to do what needs to be done."

Kolen began to give specific instruction. "For tonight, let's rotate scouts and keep watch for any activity that might come before morning. Then tomorrow we'll gather all the people to finalize how we'll defend the camp. Ryese, you be in charge of designing other weapons and making them. Eliot might remember some ideas from the

Ancients' books that he saw when very young. I will set up the rotation and then the rest of us must get some sleep." Kolen rose to leave, the others following as he spoke the Unidan blessing, "May The One have His way,"

The council dispersed with determination and faith that The One would have His way. Sandlen and Jazen went to get Karand from Ryese's Last Companion, who had taken her to play with Lornen. Their hearts were filled with sadness at the abrupt changes that had entered their lives. Once again life would change and hardships would come. Even with the strength of The One Within it would not be easy.

* * * * * *

Five mornings later, the Unidans had formed an official Council made up of the leader and his or her Last Companion, the Elders, the leaders of the scouts and all young people who had had their Becoming Day but did not have a Last Companion. Others could be added as deemed necessary. In addition, the scouts had decided on signals to alert the people who were able to fight if any Toldens approached the Edge. Some workers had gone each day to the fields armed and cautious; two people had been sent into the city to see if they could gain information as to where the captives were being held. Most of the camp was on alert, wondering what each hour might bring forth.

The sun had risen but was covered with clouds, making the air slightly crisp, as the cooler season closed upon them. A loud whistle pierced the air as Sandlen went about preparing the morning meal. She smelled the meat cooking from nearby fires. The milk she had brought up from the cold stream was in a small cup, waiting for Karand to sip with her flat cakes and eggs. Work ceased as everyone waited quietly for the next signal that would tell them if the person approaching was friend or foe. Relief flooded Sandlen's chest as she heard the signal for a friend. Maybe it was the spies who had gone into the city.

"Father, what is it?" she asked as Kolen came from his tent and headed for the square.

"I'll come and tell you as soon as I know," he promised as he kept walking. Sandlen quickly fed her daughter and ate her own food. She set some aside for Jazen who was out in the forest.

* * * * * *

Kolen came to the tent later to tell Sandlen that the two spies had returned from the city with both good and bad news. They had found where the evil king was keeping the three prisoners. It did not look like they were getting good care, but it did look possible to rescue them. Kolen had spoken to The One and tomorrow night the two would go back to the city along with two others to try to rescue the captives. The spies had also brought back word that the king was planning a raid on the Unidan camp soon. No one knew details or which day. The Unidans would have to be on the alert at all times.

Sandlen was frightened to think about anyone she knew having to fight with the Toldens. There would surely be deaths and terrible injuries. On both sides. She felt no hatred for the Toldens, just deep sadness that they didn't know The One, and didn't know how to live in peace. The rumors of life in the city were not pleasant to hear. She'd heard them since she was a child and now the rumors sounded worse. She often wondered how she could make things better for the people of the city if she had a way to talk with them. But she doubted they would listen or that she would be able to convince them of a better way with The One. It would take a miracle for the Toldens to change.

The Genesis of Atron

Her thoughts turned to questions for The One. *I am afraid, One. And I feel sad. How do the Toldens bear their pain without You? How will we bear these changes that have come to us?* She sat quietly and listened within.

Only by My hand and turning to Me, came the soft inner response. Yes, this Sandlen knew and received with reassurance. She sighed, releasing a deep breath. *And our children? Their lives will be much different than ours have been. Even with Your comfort, the emotions can be strong. Help me, One. We can't know the future; don't really want to. But we know You. You never leave us or forsake us even though everything is hard and falling apart.* She continued as her people before her had done when faced with difficult times: she said His truth and clung to His hope with faith. *Thank you, One, that you are faithful to meet me no matter the pain.* Though her feelings did not completely subside, Sandlen's heart rested as she focused her mind on The One.

* * * * * *

Sandlen woke the next morning with a heavy heart. Her thoughts from the day before about the awful life in Tolden had plagued her throughout the night. It seemed that The One was speaking within her saying that she should go to Tolden with the scouts who were planning to rescue the captives held there. She was not certain what Jazen's reaction would be or what the Elders would say. *And what about Karand?* she thought. *It's very unusual for young mothers to be put into any form of danger.*

Is this You, One? Is this what You are saying? The quiet voice she knew well responded to her query—

Trust Me, My Daughter. Listen, obey, and trust Me. I give you the desires of your heart.

Trusting His voice, Sandlen went to find Jazen.

* * * * * *

Darkness fell over Atron's forests, the colors fading as the sun dropped behind the horizon. Soon the moon would rise. The rescue party gathered their weapons and supplies, preparing to leave for the Tolden city. The Elders appealed to The One for their safe return-- accompanied by the three captives.

Sandlen spoke to The One within as she thanked Him for her time with Jazen. It had gone well as they discussed her leading from The One and consulted Him together. Trusting Him in such an unusual way would be difficult, but the turning to Him in difficult times was part of what made the Unidans who they were. Stepping out against feelings and reasoning was a true test of faith. It was easy to believe the things that were sensible. After sharing their thoughts with the Elders, they had agreed that Sandlen could be part of the rescue party.

Now Sandlen, and the other members of the rescue team, led by Ryese, crouched behind large bushes at the outskirts of the Edge, watching the path that led to the nearest Tolden gate. Her Tazor was unsheathed, her face was darkened with soot and her Father's Sedat was hooked to her belt. She, Ryese and two others were waiting for the crescent moon to rise a bit more in order to have a little light to find their way through the city. They hoped for just enough moonlight to see without being seen.

With the help of the two advance searchers, Ryese had drawn a map to the small abandoned house where the Unidans were being held. The two scouts reported that there was only one guard watching them at night and the team hoped this would still be true. Peering through the bushes, Ryese was watching the space between the trees and the city wall with his Tazor in hand and a coil of hide rope over his

The Genesis of Atron

shoulder. As soon as the path was clear and the guard patrolling the gate turned a corner, Ryese saw their chance and gave the signal for the group to make a run for the gate. He quickly pulled the latch, holding the gate open while everyone rushed through and ducked behind the nearest shop. Just as he saw the returning guard's shadow, he quietly closed the gate. No one was about this time of night as the streets on this side of the town were deserted-- late night-life abounded in a different area of the city.

Dodging in and out of shadows, they followed the map, stopping to hide behind a shed next door to the captives' house. Ryese signaled the others to stay hidden while he went to look in the windows and one of the other scouts checked the perimeter of the house.

Inside, only one guard was nodding in a chair close to the door of the one-room house. A small oil lamp sat on the floor, casting a dull light around the room. Ryese saw the three Unidans leaning against the wall in one corner, their hands bound behind their backs, cloths in their mouths. He could barely make out two other figures huddled in the corner across from the Unidans. The guard began to snore.

While making their plan that morning, the rescuers had hoped to be able to storm the door and overcome the guard. It was an added blessing from The One that he was sleeping. The other scout met Ryese by the window, signaling that all was clear. They crept to the corner of the house and motioned the others to join them.

Sandlen was nervous as she darted across the space between the shed and the house. But she trusted The One. She had no idea why He had sent her on this mission. When He chose to show her, she would know. Meanwhile, she kept her attention on the task at hand.

Ryese whispered softly, telling the four how they would enter the house. The three men would push in the door and grab the guard.

While two were tying him up, the other would check on the people in the other corner. Sandlen would go to the Unidans and set them free with her Sedat.

"Uuuggh!" groaned the guard as he hit the floor, feeling his chair fly out from under him. "What?" And then silence. When he awoke he would find himself gagged and tightly bound, feet to hands behind his back.

Across the room, Sandlen sliced the ropes binding her friends and tore the filthy rags from their mouths.

"Are you hurt?" she asked. "Will anyone else come to check on you tonight?"

"No, we're alright, all things considered. We've had water and bread, but that's all."

"No one else comes here during the night," the other Unidan added. "This is the only guard at night."

"Can you walk?" Sandlen asked. "Let me help you stand."

The three captives stood on wobbly legs and began to get the circulation moving again. As Sandlen was sharing her water with them and digging in her bag for some dried meat, across the room in the other corner she heard weeping and soft conversation. She steadied one of the Unidans as he started towards the other side of the room.

"Come, Sandlen. You must meet our new friends. During the day, we've grown to know each other while the guards wandered around outside."

Sandlen picked up the oil lamp and carried it closer to the two people sitting with Ryese and the scout. It was a Tolden woman and a

The Genesis of Atron

young Tolden girl, both thin and dirty, dressed in ragged shirts and pants, the girl's face streaked from the tears running down her cheeks.

"These two have been here longer than our friends," Ryese explained as Sandlen knelt beside the woman. "The girl is her daughter. Apparently Unidans are not the only ones whom the Toldens take captive."

Sandlen heard Ryese's anger and disgust.

"I am so sorry for what you've been through," she said, touching the woman's shoulder. "What can we do to help?"

The woman looked at Sandlen, her eyes strong with determination. "We want to help you," she said firmly. "Your captive friends have been telling us about your One, about life in Unidan and your desire to see your people reunited with ours somehow. Listening to their stories has given us hope. We don't understand, but we want to know more."

The young girl nodded as she sat up straight, wiped her face on her sleeve and managed to smile at Sandlen and the others.

Sandlen's eyes widened in surprise when she heard the woman's response and saw the girl's smile. "How do you want to help us?" Sandlen asked. "I can't imagine what you could do to help us."

"As I've listened these few days to your friends talk and watched how they interacted with the guard and each other, something stirred in my heart, something I've never felt before. I don't know anything else to call it except 'hope.'" The woman had to pause for a moment as her voice caught.

"My daughter and I were brought here because we were caught talking to a Unidan in the grain fields. It's forbidden to listen to their tales. The King hates everything Unidan."

The Genesis of Atron

"I've heard life was difficult here," Sandlen replied kindly, "that some don't have enough to eat, that many live in fear and worry about the future."

"That is true. And it can be worse for the children if something happens to their parents. Many are left to find their way on the streets." The woman sighed with the weight of it all. Sandlen could see her trying to find words for the thoughts she'd been having there in the dark house the last few days.

"We want to be your eyes and ears here in Tolden," the woman said to the rescuers. "I know others who are not afraid to listen to your stories even though it is forbidden. Some are tired of the way our life is here in the city."

The woman's words were hard to grasp. Before Sandlen could speak she continued, "If you will send some of your people to live here, to tell us more about your One and how we can work together to reunite all of Atron, we will do whatever we can to help."

Sandlen's heart began to thud against her chest. Kneeling on the floor of a filthy, tumble-down house in the outskirts of Tolden, listening to a Tolden ask to know about The One and offer help to the Unidans was more than she could have imagined. She sat back on her heels almost in shock.

Could this be what you sent me here for, One? To show me this one who wants to know more about You? You heard my desire to see changes in the Tolden city when I could not see a possibility of anyone even wanting to listen. And here is not just one, but her daughter and others they know of. Thank You, Dear One.

Sandlen looked at Ryese, her face beaming. She turned to the woman and took the woman's hand in one of hers and the girl's in the

2009 Barbara Moon

The Genesis of Atron

other. "You are going to help us!" She said. "And we are going to help you! It's almost too much to take in. It's amazing how our One works—in ways we cannot even imagine, much less plan or figure out."

"I don't know quite what you are saying there, but perhaps someday I will," the woman replied, smiling at Sandlen's enthusiasm. "I only know that my heart stirred at hearing the words of your friends."

The woman began to get up from the floor, extending a hand for Ryese's help. The girl stood with her and they both stretched their cramped limbs. "I believe we better go now and find a different place to talk. I want your people to know where to find us."

Everyone nodded in agreement as they turned to leave. Ryese and the other scouts checked the guard's ropes before they left. As the three women went out the front door, Sandlen said to her new friends, "And, please, tell me your names. I am Sandlen, Companion to Jazen and daughter of Kolen, the leader of Unidan."

"I am Cresta," the woman answered, "and this is my daughter, Tylina."

* * * * * *

The rescue party and the released captives returned to Unidan before the trussed-up guard awoke and the moon set. Before morning, word had spread around the camp about the two Toldens who wanted to know The One and who wanted to help their people. The last thing the two women had told Ryese and the others was that the king was planning a raid on the Unidan camp and it could happen any day. Discovering the prisoners missing would surely add to his fury.

Every Unidan was on high alert as the sun peeked over Atron's horizon and broke through the trees sending the shadows on the run. Extra scouts were stationed at the Edge, having just started their rotations right before dawn. Kolen and Jazen were high in the trees watching for any movement. Other scouts were scattered around in a semicircle, in or behind trees, crouching behind rocks or bushes, covering the entire area with watchful eyes. As the sun rose higher, Jazen saw some movement just past the Edge markers. He sounded the signal that was barely distinguishable from the awakening birds. But the other scouts caught it and passed it on. When it reached the camp, everyone knew their part. Some would join the scouts to fight; some would stay with the children. The older men would protect the camp should any enemies break through.

Upon hearing the signal, the Participants picked up their Tazors or the bows and arrows that Ryese had designed. Some took sharpened sticks for spears. They crept silently out towards the Edge ready to help the others.

ZHWWWWT! A blast from a Tolden Tazor lit up the air. It fell short of its mark, but gave the signal that all their men had been waiting for. They were coming to Raid the Unidan camp and had spotted one of the scouts. Unknown to them, the scout had purposefully allowed them to spot him in order to choose the time and place for their encounter.

Soon both sides were firing bright piercing energy blasts from their Tazors. But it didn't take long for shock to flood the Toldens' faces as they felt the burn of a Unidan Tazor and began to see their people falling to the ground, burnt by blasts that came from a distance. How could the Unidans hit their marks from so far away? And what were these small pointed sticks flying through the air and taking down their men?

The Genesis of Atron

With surprise, superior weaponry and The One on their side, the Unidans brought the battle to a quick end; the Toldens never penetrating very far past the Edge. The Toldens finally turned to run, picking up their wounded as they left, beaten and unsure they would ever want to return for a Raid in the near future. The Unidans cheered as they saw the raiders leaving, while back in the camp relief showed on the faces of everyone hearing the happy cry. Though outnumbered, they had fought better than the Toldens, bringing hope that perhaps the king's plans may not be as easy to pull off as he thought.

As the woods quieted, Jazen began looking for Kolen. Others were taking care of the casualties from both sides, while others started back to the camp with any wounded Unidans. Kolen did not answer when Jazen called his name. *There he is,* Jazen said to himself, spotting Kolen on the ground and breaking into a run. As he neared where Kolen lay, his heart skipped a beat. *He's hurt badly.*

Kolen lay on his side, facing away from Jazen. Jazen knelt beside his Companion's father and gently turned him over, feeling the wet sticky blood on his fingers as he touched Kolen's side.

Oh, No! Jazen dropped his head to his chest and moaned. *Oh No! One!*

Kolen was mortally wounded.

CHAPTER FIVE

Karand's light brown hair hung past her shoulders. Today it was loose from its braid, falling over her face as she helped her mother make cheese. Her brow was furrowed in deep thought about the first Raid, the lost Dome and her people's desire to reunite with the

Toldens. Her blue eyes were not focused on the task at hand that she could almost do in her sleep, but instead were distant and shaded.

Sandlen noticed that Karand was preocupied, but did not press her to talk, waiting for her to speak if she desired to. They worked quietly, straining the cheese.

Karand did not remember the first Raid or that day when her Grandfather Kolen was killed. Father didn't talk about it very often, but she'd heard stories of that time. She knew that her father had been the one to find Grandfather and carry him back to the camp. Since that time there had only been three other Raids from the Tolden city. The superior skills of the Unidans coupled with their dependence on The One had discouraged the Tolden leaders from making very many attempts. The Unidan scouts were always on the alert, guarding the Edge around the forest that separated Unidan and Tolden. As the years passed, the whole camp had grown more determined to find a way to reunite the people of Atron, a sure way to end the possibilities of a Raid.

Most of the camp believed that finding the old Dome would help reunite the people, but the other parchment half had never been found and there were strong rumors about the dangers of going into the Beyond without it. The Unidans were certain that the Toldens would come back to The One if His books were found and they could know that He was real. Many Toldens had forgotten the history of Atron, but if they could see the Dome and its contents, perhaps more would change. There was a small pocket of Toldens who tried to help, but they mostly worked in secret, having to be very careful with whom they talked.

As Sandlen finished pouring the last of the cheese into the holders, Karand finally spoke. "Mother, I'm going to find Lornen and see if he wants to go hunting."

The Genesis of Atron

"Thank you for helping with the cheese, Dear One. Enjoy your time with Lornen. Perhaps he can help you with whatever is troubling you."

As they both went to the stream to wash their hands, Karand told her mother what she was thinking about.

"I was just thinking about the day Grandfather was killed and how things changed again after that. If only we could find the lost Dome. . ." Karand dried her hands on a cloth then ran her fingers through her long hair, re-braided it and tied the end.

"I understand those feelings, Daughter. We can talk more if you want to. I will see you this evening."

"Thanks, Mother. I know your heart desires and feels this, too." Karand stooped to pick up her Tazor and her pack, following the path towards Lornen's tent.

* * * * * *

After finding Lornen, the two set off towards the western forest. Both were adept at the use of the Tazor and both enjoyed trekking through the forest to hunt or explore. Talking with Lornen had revived Karand's usual cheerful attitude and they were chattering about how hard it was to wait four more seasons for their Becoming Day when they would become full Participants, able to fight if there were a Raid on their camp. At fourteen seasons that seemed like forever to the two young people. They were eager to help the find the lost Dome and see the people of Atron reunited.

Talk of being a full Participant brought Lornen to his other favorite subject that they often discussed only when alone. He wanted to try to

The Genesis of Atron

find the Dome without the other half of the parchment. It was a dream they shared with no one else.

"I think we should go ahead and try to find the Dome by ourselves," Lornen said to Karand as they walked. "It would be such a great thing to find a way to bring our people back together and end the threat of any more Raids."

"That is a worthy goal, My Friend," answered Karand. "We've joked about it many times. After my heavy heart this morning, it seems even more worthy."

Karand stopped on the path and turned to look at her best friend. "My heart races at the hope of bringing our people back together, but it also races at the fear of going into the Beyond. We would have to go into the Beyond, you know."

"I'm willing to take the risk," Lornen assured her. "Do you think we could do it?" He raised his eyebrows and cocked his head questioningly. His dark curly hair hung below his ears and over his forehead. His brown eyes twinkled mischievously as he reminded Karand, "We both love challenges."

"That is so true," Karand smiled, continuing to consider Lornen's challenge. "We would have to find a way to get a head start. As soon as someone notices we're missing, they'll try to find us."

"You're right," he said, thinking of another question, taking the discussion farther than they ever had before. "Where would we begin? I only know the Dome is somewhere across the big river, out there in the Beyond."

"We can head for the river first thing and then decide what to do next after we cross," Karand suggested. The dream was taking shape--the more they conspired, the more excited they got.

"We could leave early one morning when we're supposed to be in the fields," Lornen added. "Our fathers wouldn't wonder about us until way up in the evening. And we could leave a note that they would find later in the day."

Karand began to walk along the path again, her mind churning and calculating as the anticipation built. *What would we have to take with us? How will we cross the river? How many days will it take? We can hunt on the way and find water--streams are all over the forests. We can do this.*

"Alright," she said aloud as they neared the treeline. "I'm willing. Let's finalize our plans and decide which day to go."

"I can't believe it! We're actually going to do this!" Lornen exclaimed. "Yes!"

Karand grinned at his enthusiasm as they quietly entered the forest. She poked Lornen's arm. When he glanced over at her, he saw mirrored in her eyes and her smile what he was already visualizing--how glad everyone would be when they knew that he and Karand had found a way to the Dome.

Neither was thinking one thought about any danger they'd heard about.

* * * * * *

Karand and Lornen had been gone for several hours. They had cut around the large grain fields north of the Tolden city's walls and headed for the big river. They had chosen a path that led through the forest in order to keep from being spotted so easily. Each carried a small pack containing a cloak, some dried meat, some cheese and cold corn cakes. They had a flint for making fire and utensils for cooking or eating out of; Lornen had a small hatchet. A hide of water was strapped to the outside of their packs, their Tazors sheathed at their waists. Each had a Sedat tucked into their belts.

The sun was higher now and the forest overhead made shadows as they wove through the trees and bushes. There were a few small trails made by animals foraging for food or trying to find water. The two chattered happily as they wondered and talked about what adventures might lay ahead. They were still not certain how they would cross the big river when the time came. But as is so often the way of young people, they expected to solve the problem when it arose. It seemed that in the face of their zeal to help their people, they had forgotten much of the elders' teachings.

"I hear the river," Karand announced, breaking into a run up a small rise. Neither traveler had ever been this far from camp.

"Yes, and I," said Lornen, running to catch up. Running down the other side of the small hill, there was the river a short distance in front of them, wide and strong, rushing swiftly over large rocks that occasionally protruded within the foam.

* * * * * *

Jazen finished cutting his last load of firewood and left the woods, dragging the sled back to camp. The sun was on its way down for the evening, casting bright oranges and pinks across Atron's western sky. As Jazen came into the camp, he passed his friend, Ryese, greeting him with a wave. He saw Sandlen returning to their tent with water from the stream. They greeted each other with a smile and a kiss on the cheek.

The Genesis of Atron

"I want to clean up downstream before we eat," Jazen said as he began unloading the wood. "The day was warm."

"You have plenty of time, My Love," Sandlen assured him as she began to prepare the meal.

"Where is Karand?" Jazen asked as he stacked the wood.

"She and Lornen went to the grain fields for the day," answered Sandlen. "Ryese was with them." Lornen's father Ryese was one of the scouts that often went to the grain fields to help watch for Toldens who might try to attack as they worked.

"Sandlen," Jazen said with alarm. "I just passed Ryese as I came back to camp and they were not with him. Where are the children?" Both parents dropped what they were doing and ran towards Ryese's tent.

"Ryese! Are the children with you?" The fear was evident in Jazen's voice as he called his friend.

Ryese hurried out of the tent. "What is it, Jazen? Sandlen?"

"Karand and Lornen were supposed to be working all day in the fields. She's not here."

"I thought Lornen was going hunting in the western forest out towards the old cave." Now Ryese shared their concern. "He's not here either."

"Who else was in the field today?" Sandlen asked. "Please call everyone together. Maybe someone saw them."

The men gathered everyone in the meeting square to listen to what little anyone knew. One of the scouts reported seeing the two young people going east out of the camp. He had wondered why they were going that way to hunt, but didn't give it much thought.

Jazen and Ryese knelt to speak to The One. They had no idea why the two young people would go off by themselves. Everyone knew the dangers of wandering anywhere near the city or out towards the Beyond. What if they had gone into the Beyond?

The group sensed that The One was directing them towards the Beyond, towards the river. Going by what the scout had seen, they decided to begin at that place in the forest. The scout and several others made up their packs to go with Jazen and Ryese to find a trail. "The One will direct us," Jazen assured his Last Companion.

"We will speak to Him on your behalf," Sandlen replied, "and ours, as we wait. Only He knows where they are and why they went." Sandlen took a deep breath, knowing all she could do was wait and trust.

* * * * * *

The wayward travelers were looking at the river and looking at the sky. How much time did they have before dark? They were still not sure how to get across the river and for some time they had been debating the question. Lornen wanted to go across holding on to a log. He thought they could float diagonally until they reached the other side. Karand wanted to walk north and find a narrower place to cross. The day was certainly warm enough to swim, but they knew all their supplies would get wet and what might happen then? The impulsivity that began this adventure was catching up with them as they took the time to think through their next step. They had eaten part of the food from their packs and enjoyed some cold clear water and were now sitting on the grassy bank throwing rocks and sticks into the water.

The Genesis of Atron

"Maybe this was not such a good idea after all," Karand said quietly. "Maybe we should go back."

"You're probably right," Lornen agreed reluctantly. "I didn't know the river was this big and fast."

"Should we wait until morning?" Karand wondered aloud. "It took us several hours to get this far."

"That seems like a good idea. We can make a fire and wait until dawn. The moon was full last night so we'll have plenty of light."

As the sun slowly lowered, they began to gather wood and small sticks to make a fire, setting up at the edge of the trees. The season was warm and their cloaks would be sufficient for the coming night air. Karand set a pot to boil for some tea. Lornen collected more wood and refilled their hides with water.

As a few stars began to twinkle here and there, the smell of their wood smoke rose above the trees into the darkening sky. The fathers and scouts from Unidan had made good time by jogging through the forest. Their pace was double that of Lornen and Karand, and it had not taken long to pick up the trail. Soon after the fire crackled, Ryese smelled the smoke.

"We are near!" he exclaimed with relief. The men picked up their pace.

* * * * * *

"What's that I smell?" barked one of the king's scouts as he and three other hunters walked near the river downstream from Karand and Lornen.

The Genesis of Atron

"Smells like someone has a fire nearby," one hunter growled suspiciously. "Who would be out here unknown to us?'

"Follow me," the scout demanded. "We're going to find out."

The four men crept towards the smoke they could now see rising above the trees. As they drew closer they could see the red and orange flames in the fire pit. The leader peered through the undergrowth seeing only two young Unidans huddled there under their cloaks. *Very odd*, he thought.

Not one to miss an opportunity to help his king find more workers for the fields, the scout signaled to his men that they would take the young people by surprise.

"Don't move! Don't touch your Tazors!" the scout yelled as he stepped through the bushes.

Karand and Lornen froze with terror, their eyes wide, their mouths gaping. There before them stood four Toldens with Tazors drawn and bows pulled. Karand could feel her heart pounding, her hands stiffening. Lornen did not move. What could he do?

"Get up! You're coming with us!" The scout pointed his Tazor at the two on the ground.

"Where are you taking us?" Lornen squeaked with fright.

"Shut up, Unidan. We don't have to tell you anything. You're on our land. Now get up!"

Lornen started to rise, taking hold of Karand's arm to help her. Just as they got to one knee, a Tazor blasted from the trees. ZHWWWT! The leader fell to the ground, smoke coming from the sleeve of his tunic. The other three turned and dropped to their knees trying to find where the blast originated. Three more blasts of light sent the hunters' weapons to the ground, burning their hands. They screamed.

Jazen and Ryese stepped from the trees, their Tazors pointed at the four Toldens. "Don't move or it will be more than your hands!" ordered Ryese. The other Unidans moved in to pick up the dropped weapons, keeping an eye on the four. Taking out hide strips, they bound the four men's hands behind their backs, and then tied their feet together.

"Are you two hurt?" Jazen asked, turning to Karand and Lornen The young people jumped up and ran to their fathers, falling into their strong arms. Jazen hugged Lornen tightly while Karand buried her face in her father's chest.

"Oh, Father. We were so scared. Thank you. Thank you, One." Karand began to cry with relief.

"Yes, Father," Lornen said to Ryese. "You saved us. We didn't know what we were doing. We were very foolish."

"You can tell us the whole story on the way back." Jazen said to them both as they gathered their packs. "I don't want to stay here another minute."

"The moon will be enough light to get us closer to home," Ryese agreed. "Come. Let's go."

Taking the Tolden Tazors and bows, the Unidans turned to leave. Jazen told the hunters, "You are blessed, as were your ancestors before you, that we do not take killing lightly. Stay away from our people, especially our young ones. You can find your way back without weapons after you sleep here."

"Ryese, kick out the fire so they can feel a little cold tonight and give some thought to still being alive because of The One." Ryese and one of the other Unidan scouts doused the fire and scattered the embers.

As the sun went down behind the trees, the Unidans set off through the forest following their own trail. The rising moon made enough light for them to wind back towards their camp. Everyone was exhausted, but the consensus was to get as far away as they could before making a camp for the night.

* * * * * *

Karand and Lornen sat meekly by the fire pit. The rescue party had finally stopped after a few hours' walk, making a small fire where they could make some tea and stave off the darkness. Each had eaten cold food from their packs, washing it down with hot tea. Jazen turned to his daughter. "Well, now, would you two like to explain to us what you've been up to?"

Karand glanced at Lornen. This was going to be very difficult. "We were trying to find a way to the old Dome, Father," she managed to say. "We've talked about many times about how wonderful it would be to go there, and we decided to go by ourselves."

"It was mostly my idea," Lornen offered. "I guess we didn't really think it through. It was very foolish."

"And almost cost you your lives," Jazen reminded them. "It was by the grace of The One that we found you in time."

The two young people were having a hard time looking at their fathers. But their training was not wasted; Karand looked up at her father's eyes. "It was very foolish, Father. I went against most of what you and the elders have taught me. I know about the parchment and the rumors about the Beyond. I didn't think. I lied to you and Mother. I was deceptive." Her voice broke as she began to weep, "And worst of all, I didn't speak to The One." Karand lowered her head, sobbing softly. Her repentance went deep.

Her father waited.

She looked up at him again with her tear-filled eyes. "I was wrong, Father. Will you forgive me?"

"Yes, My Daughter. I forgive you. I hope you've learned a lesson that will stand you throughout your life." He reached over and put his arm around her shoulders; she snuggled under his arm.

"I have, Father. I won't forget the outcome of my disobedience and foolishness. Thank you." Karand wiped her face and tried to smile. "And The One?" She paused to listen within. "He forgives me, too. Thank you, One."

It was Lornen's turn. He looked his father in the eye. "I, too, lied and deceived you, Father. I was wrong. Will you forgive me?"

Ryese nodded as he reached out to embrace his son. "I believe you will remember this in the future and realize the importance of what we tell you. I'm glad we found you both before anything terrible happened."

"I'm glad you found us, too, Father. And I thank The One," Lornen added humbly. He looked at his father. "Now I understand why we can't try to find the Dome without the other parchment half. I don't think I'll be running off without thinking again."

"Nor I," agreed Karand. "I long to see our people and the Toldens reunited and I want to find the Dome, but it's clear that it won't happen without the whole map. We were running ahead of The One, not waiting on Him. I've learned a big lesson here about it being better to follow The One and His ways."

The group rested quietly before the fire, watching the flames dance and sputter. The other rescuers spoke aloud to The One with thanksgiving for His protection and guidance. Soon the warmth of the fire and the movement of the flames made heads nod and eyes droop. Rolling snuggly into their cloaks, they all slept.

CHAPTER SIX

This was Karand's favorite time of the day. Work was finished until morning and the sunset radiated pinks and oranges across Atron's sky. Karand was now a lithe, suntanned young Unidan with her light brown braid hanging almost to her waist. Her clear blue eyes, sparkled with intelligence and joy. Her dark pants were tucked into soft boots and her shirt was dyed green and stitched with white. A Tazor hung in its sheath at her waist. The carved handle of a Sedat protruded from her right boot. Just recently she'd become a full-fledged Participant at her Becoming Day, carrying in her heart a passion for the Unidan Cause to reunite the people of Atron and return to the Dome.

Karand entered the tent where her mother sat working on some cloaks for her and her father. The cooler season was right around the corner and the whole camp was preparing for the chilly days that would follow.

Hi, Mother," Karand said absently, sitting down on a large cushion. As was her tendency now and then, she was deep in thought.

"Greetings, Daughter," Sandlen replied looking up from her sewing. Karand remained quiet, distracted by her thoughts. Sandlen returned to her task.

Being with her mother was one of Karand's favorite places to be. At her mother's knee Karand had heard the stories of how things had changed after the first Tolden Raid and her grandfather Kolen was killed. Sandlen had passed down to her daughter the passion she carried to find the old Dome, The One's Books and to see Atron's people reunited. When together, the two often talked about what they had come to call "the Cause." They laughingly revisited the time when a much younger Karand had even tried to help the Cause by venturing out with her friend Lornen to find the Dome by themselves. A foolish, youthful venture had almost cost them their lives, but had turned out well thanks to The One and their fathers, and Karand had learned a huge lesson that she could now laugh about.

Karand had nothing but loving memories of the seasons growing up with her parents, even when she made mistakes like trying to find the Dome. They had prepared her well through the years leading up to her Becoming Day. She looked back on that day with joy, standing before her mother and father and all the people as she gave her pledge with Lornen, her best friend, her First Companion. Lornen had been most faithful to help and support her as he'd promised during the ceremony.

Thinking about her Becoming Day pledge made Karand think about the change the Elders had made in it after that first Raid. They had added a new phrase to the First Companions' promise. After the addition, when the young people called themselves Participants it meant more than just being an adult—it meant those who could fight for the Cause as well as work for it.

It's so sad to me that the Elders had to add that phrase to the old pledge, Karand thought, *but I know it was necessary.* She heard it in her mind-- *'I promise to do my best to protect you in battle.'* As she thought of that day at her ceremony, she finished the rest of the pledge made between First Companions, saying it softly to herself-- ". . . to sacrifice myself for your good if necessary; to speak the truth to you at all times, listen to your admonitions and to practice with you the openness necessary to live closely with another."

"What are you mumbling there, Dear One?" asked Sandlen, looking up again.

"I was remembering my Becoming Day and how the Elders added the new phrase before my group made their pledges. I was saying the whole thing aloud."

"Yes, many things changed, didn't they, during those years before your Day," her mother said sadly. "You and Lornen grew up together in the changes that came to Atron. It drew you very close to each other."

"That's true, Mother. Though we don't feel the love to be Last Companions, our love is strong. And we both still long for the Cause to happen in our life-time, just as we did that day we sneaked off to find the Dome. That longing draws and holds us together."

"I know that's your desire as it is mine and your father's. To find the lost parchment half and the electrokey, and go to the old Dome— find the One's books that are lost— that would be the most wonderful event I can imagine. I would not be able to contain myself. And to think it might help us see the people of Atron reunited as they were in the beginning—that would be as wonderful. Perhaps you and Lornen will experience it."

Sandlen's hands stilled from her sewing for a moment. "I don't sense from The One that your father and I will see it," she added sadly, "though that doesn't in any way diminish my passion for it to happen."

Karand saw the look of sadness in her mother's eyes. It was often there, since that awful day of the first Raid when Grandfather Kolen had been killed. Karand knew the look, but she also knew that her mother suffered well in her sadness and did not allow it to change her or to change how she loved and interacted with everyone. Karand didn't remember that Raid, but she lived with the effects it had on her people. Karand sometimes wished she could remove that look of sadness which often haunted her mother's eyes.

Scooting over to sit by her mother, Karand leaned towards her and gave her a hug. The two sat quietly drawing comfort from each others' embrace. In a moment Karand whispered their old Unidan blessing that now, because of the Raids, had a new meaning associated with the Cause, "May The One have His way."

Sandlen answered with the new response, "May it be soon."

She raised her head and smiled at her daughter. "The One *will* have His way in *His* time, of that I am sure," she added. "He assured me of that when I met Cresta and Tylina those many years ago."

"Yes, I know," Karand smiled back at her, squeezing her tightly. "But I love hearing reassurances said aloud, don't you?"

"Oh, yes," Sandlen agreed. "I never tire of hearing The One's truth."

The One's guidance and strength kept the Unidans stable now as it always had before and after that awful day. Right before the first Raid, the scouts had managed to free the captives taken from the grain

The Genesis of Atron

field; in fact, Sandlen had been part of the mission. Through unusual circumstances guided by The One that day, they had met the Tolden woman, Cresta, and her young daughter, Tylina. Now and then, through the years these two had secretly helped the Unidans by passing along important information concerning other Raids and edicts put out by the king. Through their channels, some Toldens had become more open to hearing about The One.

Meeting the woman who wanted to help them made a terrible event more bearable for Sandlen and her people. If not for that meeting and the Unidan's dependence on The One and His ways, the Unidans might have gone the way of the Toldens and just given up and turned away from Him.

Karand only knew from her parents' stories of the pain and horror that had come upon Unidan that day. Never had a Unidan killed another person. Never had the people dreamed of having to fight others and defend their land. But the people had risen to the need, becoming skillful warriors ready to defend and fight when necessary.

She knew from the Elders' teachings that a Unidan—her great, great grandfather Vandlyn-- had been killed by a Tolden long ago. That was one of the reasons the Toldens and Unidans were enemies and why the Dome was lost now. The parchment her mother had in a trunk was said to be part of a map that would lead the people back to the Dome. But during the fight long ago, the parchment was split in two. The other half that would make it possible to find the Dome was lost, and they couldn't go to the Dome without the missing parchment half. Karand and Lornen had learned that lesson well.

Karand knew how the loss of her father had driven Sandlen to a deeper focus with The One and her fierce determination to see the people of Atron reunited. In spite of all the evidence from rumors and occasional Raids, this distant relationship with the Tolden women had

2009 Barbara Moon

The Genesis of Atron

given Sandlen hope that more of the Toldens in the city would come to know The One. She had pushed through her sadness of losing her Father, even using the pain, to help instill in Karand the importance of the Cause. They often talked of what it might be like to see The One have His way. There were hardly words to describe how that might feel and look.

Fighting the tears that came to her eyes, Karand rose to leave. As she left the tent, her mother said, "We'll have a Council tonight in about an hour. The Elders have sensed some ideas from The One."

"I look forward to knowing what they've heard," Karand replied. "I'll be back to help you in a few minutes."

She left the tent, crossing the path to sit on the large rock that protruded out over the stream, allowing a few of the tears to roll down her cheeks as she folded her foot under her hips. The sunset was nearly complete, the colors fading to dusk. The stream gurgled and rushed over the rocks below her perch, splashing Karand lightly with cold water. The flow of the stream ran much lower now than it had when she was a child. The wonderful thunder storms and pattering rains came less often and the forest was beginning to show the effects, adding to Karand's passion for finding the lost parchment. Surely an answer to the drought could be found at the lost Dome. Wiping her eyes, she turned over on her stomach and let her hand fall into the sparkling water, her thoughts continuing along the lines of how things had changed over the years.

I love it when Mother takes out her half of the parchment and shows it to me and tells me the parts of the stories that she remembers. She has tried to pass down as many of them as she can. There's a key somewhere, an electrokey—that will open the old Dome. But we have to have the other half of the parchment to find it. Karand lazily ran her hand through the water as she pondered the stories. *I remember the day Mother allowed me to show the parchment to Lornen. I knew it was unusual to show it to anyone outside the family. But,* she smiled to herself, *Lornen is like family. He's a good man and I've trusted him with my life. He surely came through with that part of our pledge—protecting me at our first Raid together.*

I remember that day after we'd taken our pledges. The Toldens approached the Edge early that morning and the scouts signaled for the Participants to come quickly. Lornen and I were milking goats, laughing together and looking forward to Tazor practice. At the scout's signal, we jumped to our feet, knocking over one of the hides of milk as we grabbed our Tazors and ran towards the Edge.

Just as Lornen and I cautiously joined the others in the area where the scouts had seen movement, two of the King's guards stepped out from behind a tree near where we were hiding. One drew back his bow, aiming an arrow right at me. Lornen fired his Tazor at the same time he jumped in front of me. The guard fell, his arrow curving away from our position, barely missing Lornen's arm. In seconds the whole area was covered with flying arrows, spears and the noise of Tazor blasts--Lornen and I fighting back to back as we'd been trained. When it was over, both of us hoped we would never have to do that again.

Remembering the Raid turned Karand's thoughts gratefully to The One: *Thank you, One, that we haven't had very many Raids through the years. I think that's because of You and how the Toldens believe we're such amazing fighters. They don't know the secret of the Tazor—they don't know You.*

Karand's thoughts meandered in yet another direction as she squirmed to get more comfortable on her rock. *Wilden's another good man here in Unidan,* she thought. *It's fun to be with him and he loves*

The One as I do. Perhaps, One, You're saying some things to me about him. I wonder where that might go.

"Karand!" she heard Lornen call, as he walked down the path towards her. "Have you heard about the Council meeting later tonight?"

"Yes. Mother just told me." She sat up and patted the rock. "Come on up here by me."

Lornen climbed up and settled himself beside his First Companion perched on the rock. "The Elders have some ideas to discuss with everyone. I wonder what it's about."

"I don't know. Mother didn't say." Changing the subject, Karand lowered her eyes, asking softly, "Have you seen Wilden today?"

"Oh, you want to know about Wilden, do you?" Lornen answered with a deep chuckle. "And what do you want to know that for?"

"Just wondering." She glanced over at Lornen and burst out laughing at his expression. His eyebrows were raised and he had a big smirk on his face. "You know. Just wondering."

"Oohh, I don't know about that," he smiled some more. "I think it's more than wondering. You'd be interested to know that he was asking about you this afternoon, too."

"He was? What did he say? What did you say?"

"He said he was going to go sit in a tree and think about you," Lornen teased. "You know. That's what the scouts do—they sit in trees."

Karand nearly pushed Lornen off the rock they were sharing. "I ought to push you right into the water. This time of the season, that should help you show some respect."

"Go ahead and try," he dared with a grin, standing to his feet. Kandra was strong but she wasn't stupid. She knew who would land in the stream. Instead of taking his dare, she laughed out loud, jumped off the rock and ran down the path. Lornen followed her, catching up quickly.

As they scuffled on the path, the object of their mirth appeared through the trees. Wilden's rotation was finished and he was returning home for his evening meal that his mother would have saved for him. Thinking of Karand had helped pass the time he'd had to sit in that tree. And there she stood right in front of him.

"Hi! What are you two fighting about now?" Wilden inquired. "I've never seen two First Companions who love to tease each other as you two do."

Karand and Lornen laughed again as she said to Lornen, "You win. You caught me fairly. But remember, you just missed getting pushed into the water."

And to Wilden. "How was your watch this afternoon?"

"It went well and quickly I would say. And how has your day been?"

"A regular day so far. I spent some time with Mother as usual. We're having a Council tonight. They have some new plans to discuss.'

"I'll see you there," Wilden said as he continued along the path. "I want to clean up before I eat my meal." Wilden grinned at Karand and winked at Lornen as he passed them on the path.

CHAPTER SEVEN

Karand was enjoying her son's Last Companion ceremony. Her blue eyes were yet strong and bright though her hair was sprinkled with gray. She still wore it braided, but now it was twirled into a bun at her neck. Instead of her usual robe, she was wearing her Becoming Day dress that she had also worn for her own ceremony with Wilden. Today their son Handen was joining with his Last Companion, Esleda. Watching them brought to mind hers and Wilden's ceremony seasons ago. Though the times were very difficult, they'd managed a beautiful ceremony as all the people contributed what they could to help make a special joining. She missed Wilden. And their daughter Jaslen, who had also died for the Cause. She felt the prick of missing them, but as her mother had, she suffered well and did not allow the pain to interfere with her love for others nor for her passion to see a change in Tolden and win the Cause.

Her seasons with Wilden had been wonderful as they worked together to do all they could to bring about the Cause of their people. Like her mother, she carried that passion in her heart, passing it down to her son, Handen, even though it did not look promising that she might see the reuniting of Atron in her lifetime. But she never stopped asking The One for it to be so.

Her journey with The One had been full of joy and faith, though through the seasons she had lost many close to her. And the drought was worsening. Atron might die if The One did not intervene. The dying planet increased her longing to find the other half of the parchment that would lead them to the Dome. All of it--the lost books of the Ancients, The One's books, their history, a way to help the planet-- might be found there in the lost Dome. And to see the people reunited—that was her biggest longing. *I wonder what it will take for all these things to come forth,* she thought as the people's rejoicing brought her back to the ceremony.

Handen and Esleda finished their promises and came out into the crowd for hugs and congratulations. Karand rose to greet them as well. "Welcome to our family," she told Esleda. "You are as a daughter."

"Thank you, Mother. I'm honored. And I love your son. We shall serve our people and do all we can to continue your work for the Cause."

As Karand moved through the crowd greeting everyone, she spotted Lornen. How long had it been? So many seasons ago, after Sandlen and Ryese met the Tolden woman, Cresta, the Council had agreed that they should send a few Unidans to live in Tolden as spies in order to send knowledge of their activities back to the camp. That was when she and Lornen were very young, but through the years others had taken their places in order to continue to advance the Cause. Right before she and Wilden had joined, Lornen had volunteered, knowing it was not an easy choice. He was gone most of the time, though he had a tent in the camp, coming back to visit now and then.

"My Dear First Companion." Lornen's eyes lit up with joy as he embraced Karand. "A day of joy to see two young people joined together as one, as are we with The One. A blessing from Him."

"Oh, Yes," Karand responded as she pulled back to look into his eyes--the kind and wise eyes that she'd known her whole life. "Watching the two there on the platform took me back to my ceremony and life with Wilden. What fun we had and how blessed we were with our work for our families and the Cause. It went especially well, and quickly I might say, after he finally had the courage to speak his heart to me."

"Yes, I remember that day he told me he was going to think about you while on watch sitting in the trees. The One must have prodded him to take the risk of speaking to you. It wasn't long after that until you were Last Companions."

"And with your added support as my First and your help as his friend we managed to get the words spoken aloud. Thank you for both," she chuckled. Changing the subject she asked, "How is it going in Tolden?"

"It's difficult. I live alone with very little interaction with others, only occasionally seeing the Tolden helpers. I can't mix with the people except in the streets. But I listen and remember what I hear when I'm out and about. If I'm quiet, no one notices an old man." Lornen paused as if to decide how much to say. "It's not a good place for anyone. Many areas are not safe as they often take people to work in the fields against their will. Young ones steal from the shop keepers and they don't have to go to teaching time unless they want to."

"I've heard many of the rumors. We speak often to The One about you and the others there, as well as the Toldens themselves."

"Those of us living there, and especially those who have been captured and have to work in the fields, do speak out now and then of The One and the Dome. We try to keep the rumors going in spite of the opposition and the edicts against talking of the Undian ways. We hope there are some who may listen and remember pieces of what they've heard."

"I know it helps the Cause that all of you speak of a better life when you can. We may never know what seeds you plant in the hearts of the Toldens around you."

Lornen nodded in agreement. Changing the subject to other concerns he asked, "How are the people here faring with the drought? It worsens I feel. And it will get worse for you here in the camp. The city has easier access to the fields and they can use the river for irrigation."

"We struggle to get the grain and other food from the fields. For now the Toldens just watch us as long as we give them the share that their king demands. I wonder how it will be after more seasons, what it will be like for the next generation."

"The One will have His way. He will direct and provide."

Tucking their concerns away temporarily in order to enjoy the new couple, the two old friends continued to move around the celebration, speaking to and hugging all whom they met.

CHAPTER EIGHT

"Gran! Gran! Please tell me a story, and can I see your parchment?" Her long dark hair swinging loosely from side to side, Little Candra was dancing eagerly around inside her grandmother's tent waiting for an answer. Her blue eyes gleamed with the anticipation common to any child with six seasons who was waiting to do her favorite activity. She always wanted to look inside Gran's trunk or hear any stories that Gran had to tell her, even if she told the same ones over and over. "And when can I be a runner, Gran? I want to help with the Cause."

The Genesis of Atron

"Oh, My Dear One, you'll have to wait many seasons to be a runner. It's a dangerous job, but I know you'll do it well when you're old enough." Gran loved nothing more than being with Little Candra and passing on all the stories she knew of The One and Atron.

"Can I see the parchment? Just for a minute? I'll be really careful with it," Candra continued persistently. "And we can look at your Becoming Day dress, too."

"Patience, My Child. Patience. You can't be a runner yet, but yes, we can look at the parchment."

Gran smiled to herself as she went over to kneel beside her small trunk that always stood in the corner of her tent. What a joy it was to share her life and stories with Candra, the ever eager one. And Nathan, too. Two seasons younger, he was yet following Esleada around the camp, always close to Esleda or Handen. But Candra spent every spare moment with her Gran.

Karand still remembered the first time she had shown the parchment to Candra. As soon as she saw it, her eyes grew big and wide. She asked Gran with awe, "Can I show it to Joden, Gran? Please? She's my best friend. It's so strange; not like anything else I've ever seen."

Gran had quickly explained to Candra that no one else outside the family could see the parchment. "It's extremely valuable and we have to keep it hidden and protected. I will tell you some stories about it when you're older and why we must take great care of it."

Candra's eyes grew wide again, mirroring the seriousness on Gran's face. She wanted to make sure she understood. "So it's like a good secret? I don't tell anybody? Like when we're going to celebrate somebody's Becoming Day or birthing day?" Candra looked puzzled for a moment. "What about Mother and Father—or Nathan?"

Gran smiled, touching the little frown between Candra's eyes. "That's right, Precious One. You can tell Mother and Father, and Nathan when he's bigger, but no one else. Do you understand?"

"Oh, Yes, Gran!" Candra's eyes danced as she looked down again at the parchment. "That's a big 'sponsbility, isn't it? I understand. And I promise to keep the secret."

Karand was brought back to the present by Candra moving to kneel beside her, trying to be patient. There. Gran unlocked the trunk, lifted out her Becoming Day dress and laid it aside. Underneath was the soft hide that held the Unidan half of the parchment. Gran carefully unrolled the hide as Candra's eyes sparkled expectantly. She loved to touch the strange material and run her fingers along the colorful lines and words.

"Oh, Gran. It really is lovely and mysterious, isn't it? Do you think we'll ever find the other half? And what do you think the electrokey looks like? What do you think it is?" Candra took a deep breath, finding it hard to sit still, her questions tumbling over each other.

"When I grow up and have my Becoming Day and can be a Participant," she continued, "I'll go out into the Beyond and find the Dome. You can come with me. And Nathan, too."

Gran laughed out loud at Candra's excited chatter. "It has been my lifelong dream and desire from The One to find the parchment, Little One. Maybe you'll be able to find the Dome someday. But you can't go without the whole map. You know they say the Beyond is very dangerous."

"Yes, I know those stories, Gran. But what is the danger? Does anyone really know?"

"I've never heard any specifics, Dear, just rumors. Most of them come from the Tolden city. When you're older I'll tell you of a time I tested the stories and learned to listen to them even if I didn't know all the reasons."

"I love all your stories, Gran, especially new ones," Candra said as she watched Gran finish unfolding the parchment.

Gran spread the parchment out on a cushion and they went over it again, pointing at the scribbling. Without the other half, it was impossible to know what all the symbols and writing meant. As she watched Candra peer at the map trying so hard to figure it out, Karand smiled. *She may have only completed six seasons*, Karand thought, *but already she is strong in her love for The One and the Cause. Only He knows what will happen in the future, but for now we'll all continue to build His ways into her. Only He knows what shall come forth in her lifetime.*

"Your dress is very pretty, Gran." Candra said, her change of interest to the dress interrupting Karand's thoughts. "Did you help your mother make it?"

"My mother did most of the work, but I did help her. It's more traditional for the mother or other women to make the dresses for Becoming Day and Last Companion Day. It's part of their gift to the young woman, but sometimes the girl does help." Karand smoothed a wrinkle on her dress, remembering that time seasons back. "Since we wear pants and shirts or robes most of the time, the dresses are extra special."

The Genesis of Atron

"What do you think I will wear for my day?" Candra asked. "I know what Nathan will wear-- the robe passed down through the seasons that Father wore."

"Yes, that is the usual way for the boys, but you will get to decide when the day nears. It will be fun to plan your dress and see all the loving stitches that go into it."

"I like the flowers and the long sleeves on your dress," Candra said as she touched each flower lining the front. "Great grandmother Sandlen did beautiful work."

"Oh, yes she did, My Dear. She taught me as well. I loved sitting with her and talking about everything as we sewed. There are many things to learn in order to keep our families fed and clothed. And many stories to tell about The One and His ways."

"Do you miss her, Gran?"

"Yes, I miss her every day. But I know she is with The One. She would have been so proud to see you and Nathan. You have her eyes, you know."

"And yours, too!" Candra exclaimed, jumping up to leave, planting a wet kiss on her grandmother's cheek along with a big hug around her neck. "Thank you, Gran, for showing me everything again. I'm going to find Mother and Nathan. I'll be back!" That last declaration left no doubt at all in Karand's mind.

As Candra left the tent, Karand reverently folded the parchment and rolled it back into the soft hide, placing it into the trunk. Then she laid her dress back on top and closed the lid. It was very difficult to realize that one day, if things didn't change, her precious grandchildren might have to be runners and warrior Participants. She

The Genesis of Atron

often spoke with The One about such things. And what if the drought continued to worsen? What would happen to Atron then?

Because of the drought and the Tolden king's greediness, the Unidans found it necessary to smuggle grain and other food from the fields or the city. This was part of a runner's job. They went through the forest to the Edge to meet Unidans like Lornen who chose to live in the city in order to send reports back to the camp or help smuggle grain. The runners received the grain and/or message tubes that they then brought back to camp. The whole system to guard the camp and the Edge was carefully planned and carried out. The Unidans could not let down their guard for a moment.

So much has changed, Gran sighed. *But,* she whispered to The One, *You have not--You have not and never will. I'm uncertain what will happen with the drought worsening and the interactions with the Toldens so bad, but when we're afraid we'll trust in You as we always have.*

Gran got up from the trunk and moved to the fire to make some stew and flat cakes. She would need to make a trip to the cold stream where she stored her milk. And she would need some water to heat for cleaning her dishes. After the meal she would visit with Handen and Esleda and the young ones. Maybe take some sewing with her to work on. And she would ask Handen what news the latest runners had brought in.

Handen now received the message tubes and led the camp. Karand had decided to step down as leader a few seasons back and allow Handen and Esleda to take over. In Tolden each successive king since Oland had been worse than the previous. King Krall, the current leader was very cruel and very greedy. He had forced his people to build a castle for him, formed a larger army of guards and stooped to taking Unidans as captives whenever possible. But there had been few actual

Raids on the camp because of the expertise the Unidans showed with their Tazors and strategies. King Krall had no idea why he could not defeat them, but rumors raced within the city—rumors that the Unidans knew something the Toldens did not know. After the first Raid long ago, the Toldens figured out how to make the new weapons that Ryese had designed, so they relied less on their Tazors, believing they could get more distance with the arrows.

As she cooked and went about her evening chores, Karand's thoughts turned to Lornen, her old friend and First Companion. He still stayed much of the time in Tolden as one of the spies. When he returned to camp now and then, they always spent time together. He enjoyed the young ones, watching them grow and listening to their chatter. Lornen was a gentle man with a deep desire to see the Cause come about. He'd dedicated his life to helping the Cause by being obscure in Tolden. It was not easy. He had to move about with great care, always staying aware of the guards, especially when he met a runner at the Edge to send grain or a message tube back to his people.

It would be good to see Lornen again soon, Karand mused as she left the tent to go to the stream. *I trust he's well.*

PART THREE—The People of Tolden

CHAPTER ONE

Darrias was very worried about her sister. They were alone in Kaylan's suite in the castle, sitting at a small table laid out with cheese, bread and fruit. As the queen of Tolden, Kaylan wore a beautiful robe of shimmering, almost indescribable material. The colors changed as she walked and the material rustled softly around her ankles. It was said that the unusual material once belonged to Oland of the Dome and it had been brought with him when the people left the Dome long ago. Darrias wore the traditional Tolden robe woven from plants that grew in the forests around the city. She had dyed the cloth and stitched it delicately with various colors of thread. She wore her shiny black hair pulled back and tied at her neck. Her green eyes shone with intelligence and understanding. Kaylan's brown hair was streaked with auburn and matched her brown eyes—kind eyes that looked tired and worn. Years of living with Krall were taking their toll on Kaylan. If not for her lady in waiting, Tylina, she would have no one in the castle to call a friend.

Darrias and her husband, Jired were contemplating some serious actions to help Kaylan and the people of Tolden. It would be treasonous, and should they be caught, it would mean certain death.

But Krall had to be stopped; his cruelty to both his queen and his people was known throughout the city. In truth, the crown actually belonged to Kaylan by rights from their father Gerol, a descendant of Oland of the Dome, but Krall had taken over after their joining, making certain that everyone understood he was now the ruler.

Across the room from the small table, Tylina was quietly preparing some tea as the sisters spoke quietly together.

"Kaylan," Darrias pleaded touching her sister's hand, "you have to listen to us. It's getting worse and worse. Krall does nothing to help the people who are hungry, nothing to stop the young ones running loose in the streets and nothing to lessen the abuse of the Unidans. He takes advantage of every possibility to hinder or hurt them whenever possible."

"It's true as you say, Darrias," her sister answered as she took a cup from Tylina and blew across the top. After serving Darrias as well, Tylina bowed and went to her own room. "I fear him greatly--and more each day. At times I fear for my life. I worry about what my boys are learning as they watch the court, their father and the city?"

"You're right," Darrias agreed. "The influence from the court is overwhelming. There are so few Toldens who remember any good times, that I fear soon there will be none. There is little hope. Occasionally I hear talk of hope about The One of the Unidans—and occasionally I listen, but what I hear is hard to believe, and I don't really understand it."

"Yes," Kaylan mused. "Sometimes when I'm speaking my worries to Tylina, she makes comments about those Unidan stories. It's almost as if she knows more than she lets on, as if she understands them."

The Genesis of Atron

"Well, I find it hard to believe that something invisible would be interested in our worries and cares. Most people I know follow Krall's edict to stay away from such nonsense. If their One is so powerful, why doesn't he do something to help us?"

"I don't know the answers to any of this," Kaylan responded. "I just know that the people are suffering—and I fear for my children—and my life. It's almost more than I can bear.

Leaning over to hug her sister, Darrias continued, "You're right. And the children do suffer. My Brinid fears going out. She stays alone most of the time."

"And Eric," Kaylan added. "I worry the most about him. He is very different from Stephad, though I carried them together." A tear appeared in her eye as she thought of her sons. "I'm afraid already Stephad is much like his father. I often feel it's too late to see him change."

Darrias sat quietly for a moment, thinking of what she wanted to say next. She ate a thin slice of fruit from her plate.

When she was ready, Darrias leaned towards her sister and lowered her voice. "We have to do something before it's too late for all of us. Jired and I have talked about it many times. We have a plan-- but it's dangerous." She waited for Kaylan's reaction.

"It scares me to hear you talk that way," the queen replied.

"Jired wants us to overthrow Krall and return the court to you. He knows others who think as we do and who will help."

"I don't know." Kaylan's voice betrayed her fear. "What would you do with Krall and his men?"

The Genesis of Atron

"We would send them out into the Beyond and forbid them to return to this area. Jired and the others have it well planned. It would be difficult to make changes, but we all feel it's possible and worth the risks."

Kaylan sat quietly for a few moments. Part of her wanted to believe it possible to live free from Krall's abuse, but part of her felt terrified at the thought of trying to cross him. What about Eric and Stephad? What if something happened to her instead of Krall? These were troubling questions that needed consideration.

Finally, Kaylan spoke again. "I don't know, Darrias. Krall is very powerful and cruel. What if we fail?"

"Jired and I believe our plan is solid. There is much to be gained—especially for you. And for our people. They suffer daily."

"Again you are right, Darrias. My heart is troubled for all of us." Kaylan paused again, considering another question.

"What about the treasure map?" Kaylan asked. "You know how important Mother and Father said it is—how we must guard it carefully. How we must continue to pass it down the generations in case we're one day able to find the other half of the parchment that will show us how to find the lost treasure."

"Krall still doesn't know about it, does he?" Darrias asked quickly. She took a sip of her tea and ate some bread and cheese.

"Never. No one except you and me, if you've not told anyone."

"I've only told Jired," Darris replied. "He understands the importance of the secret."

The Genesis of Atron

Kaylan grew quiet, holding her warm cup as she pondered all that they'd been talking about. She looked straight at her sister. "I want to give it to you. I want you to hide it in case something goes wrong. Will you take it?"

"You know we'll do whatever will help you, Dear One. Whatever will free your mind from some worry."

Kaylan rose from her seat and went to one of her baskets. She lifted it, carrying it over to the table where Darrias sat. Removing the lid, she took out the torn parchment, laying it on the table between them. Darrias reached out a hand to touch it.

"It's so long since I've seen it," she observed. "It's so odd. . . And such a mystery. I wonder what happened back there that changed so many things—and, I wonder--what is the treasure?"

"Most all of the details have been lost through the years," Kaylan replied. "Mother told me that there's a place across the river that contains hidden treasure, but no one remembers where or what it is. And the old Dome is supposed to be out there in the Beyond somewhere--if it even exists."

"I vaguely remember that, too," Darrias said. "I don't think many people believe that it's real. Isn't it part of the forbidden stories the Unidans tell?"

"Yes I think so. And Krall does not want anyone to give credibility to their tales. He gets furious if they're mentioned."

"Well, I agreed to keep the secret mostly because it seemed important to Mother and Father," Darrias said, "but finding some lost treasure was not something I wanted to do—especially without the whole map."

The Genesis of Atron

"The map seemed so important to them that I've purposefully kept it from Krall. It was one thing I could control. But I don't think about it very often. And I look at it even less." Kaylan followed one of the lines with her finger and rubbed the split edge. "It is strange material, isn't it?" she observed.

"Yes. I remember the material from when we were young when Mother first showed it to us. She knew few details of its history either. She only knew it was very old and extremely valuable and to be passed down to the oldest child each generation."

Kaylan looked at her sister. "Will you take it?" she asked quietly. She didn't want to press Darrias. Perhaps it would be dangerous to have it in one's possession should Krall ever discover it existed.

"Yes, I will take it." Darrias was quick to answer, wanting to do all she could to help her sister. "I know Jired would agree. It's vital that Krall not find out about it. Jired and I have less visibility at court than you do. It has never been our desire to live at the court," she added.

"Thank you, My Sister. Take it in this basket as you go. It will seem to be like anything else you might carry home."

Darrias stood, preparing to leave. "One of us will send word to you when the time is right for our plan so that you will know the hour. The next time we're together, I hope to see you free." The sisters embraced, holding each other for a moment. Neither had a great amount of hope, but each felt that they must take this course for the sake of the children and the people--and to protect Kaylan.

2009 Barbara Moon

CHAPTER TWO

Eric and Stephad were supposed to be listening to the teacher with whom they had lessons each day. Eric liked listening, but Stephad liked mistreating Eric. They were twins—the first and second princes of Tolden, and Stephad never missed a moment to remind Eric that he, Stephad, was the First Prince of Tolden. After all he had twenty-three minutes on Eric's six seasons--and therefore deserving of all privileges to Eric's detriment. They both had dark wavy hair and soot brown eyes, but the sameness ended there. Eric's eyes were kind and questioning but Stephad's were sneaky and cold. Their personalities matched their eyes.

Unlike the Unidans' simple work clothing, the princes wore soft shirts and tunics decorated with colorful embroidery, flowing pants and soft slippers. Until they were old enough to learn the skills necessary for war, their days would contain little work other than teaching time.

During teaching time, the teacher was not very successful at keeping Stephad in line when he determined to harass his brother or misbehave in any other way. After all, he was the prince. Eric was glad when the teacher finally dismissed them. He ran through the castle to his mother's rooms. Stephad went to find the king.

Eric's favorite part of the day was when he was with his mother or with Tylina. Tylina had been in the castle since his mother was a child and she loved him almost as much as his mother did. He loved to sit with her and listen to her read, her soft, kind voice soothing away the jabs from his brother. Tylina's red hair, peppered with grey, was fading as she aged, but it still hung in long curls around her face, framing her brown eyes that always shone with love towards Eric and his mother. Besides from his mother and Tylina, around the court it

The Genesis of Atron

was unusual to observe these qualities and Eric basked in the kindness he received from both of them. As he entered the room, he noticed his mother sitting on her large cushions, staring out the window. She appeared very sad.

"Mother." Eric quietly approached his mother's side. "What is it? Why are you so sad?"

"It's many things, My Son. Things you are too young to bother with."

"Will you tell me when I'm older?" he asked as she made room for him on her cushion and pulled him down to sit beside her.

"When you're older and it is time." Kaylan placed a kiss on his head. "Do you want something to eat? There's cheese and fruit on the table," she added, pointing to the table. "Or Tylina can bring you something else."

"Where is Tylina? Maybe she would play with me."

"I can call her," his mother said as she rose to ring the bell that would call Tylina to their room.

When Tylina appeared, Kaylan asked her to take Eric outside. Tylina knew the queen's worries and quickly noticed the concern in her voice. They spent many hours together speaking of things that few others knew.

"It's always my pleasure to be with Prince Eric, My Lady," she said and took Eric's hand with a smile.

"And when he goes to bed this evening, I have some things I need to tell you," Kaylan said seriously.

The Genesis of Atron

"I understand, My Lady." Turning to Eric, Tylina said playfully, "Let's go, Big Man. What would you like to do outside?"

CHAPTER THREE

Eric and Stephad were settled and asleep for the night. King Krall was about his business, doing whatever it was that might please him at a given moment. Tylina entered Kaylan's suite to find her preparing for bed. Her untouched evening meal sat on the table. "I am here, My Lady."

"Come, sit, My Friend," Kaylan said gesturing to the floor cushions. "It has been a difficult day and I have things to tell you. My heart is heavy with worry and fear." Tylina could see the burden weighing on her mistress's shoulders. It was often there. Kaylan continued. "It seems that Darrias, Jired and some others are planning an insurrection against the king. She told me about it this morning. They will send me word when it's to take place." The look on Kaylan's face was heart breaking. "Tylina," she said, "I'm afraid."

"I understand." Tylina laid her wrinkled had gently on her queen's. "What can I do for you?"

Kaylan could hardly speak. Her voice caught as she began, "I want you to promise me that if something happens to me that you will take care of Eric." She tried to collect herself. "I fear more for him than I do for Stephad. It seems to me that Stephad will follow his father and there is not much I or anyone else can do. But Eric. . ." Kaylan could hold back no longer. She broke down in tears, sobbing deeply. Tylina waited quietly. In a few moments Kaylan took a cloth and wiped her face.

"I don't know what's going to happen, Tylina. I've lost hope." Kaylan began to cry again. Tylina could see her pain and fear. It was not an easy place to be. Kaylan looked up again, sniffling and wiping her eyes. "I fear for Eric's future. I don't want him to become like his father. If I know you will be there to influence him if I'm gone, then I can face this easier."

"I won't say your talk is nonsense, My Lady, though I wish I could. But I can say that I promise to care for Eric and teach him kindness and love, in spite of this court around him, should something happen to you." Tylina did not want to think of such a possibility coming true, but she saw the pain that Kaylan carried and her need to have a plan.

"Your promise helps settle my heart," Kaylan replied with a deep sigh of relief. "I know you will remember this conversation and your promise if that day ever comes. Thank you, My Friend."

Tylina rose from the cushions, wishing there was more she could do to help her mistress. It was very difficult to watch Kaylan live in fear and worry so much when Tylina knew that knowing The One could make a difference. *All I can do is speak to Him again on her behalf the same as I've been doing all these years,* she whispered to herself as she went to her room.

CHAPTER FOUR

The world was dark and extremely frightening.

There was no light; no people.

No noise.

The Genesis of Atron

Little Brinid, raven hair spilling over her face, was cowering in a corner of her small room, knees to her chin, green eyes wide with fear, wondering when Mother and Father would return. They sometimes went out without her, but never for this long. Her six seasons were not enough to help her contain the fear.

Several days earlier Brinid had noticed that Mother and Father seemed preoccupied and sad. She'd overheard them talking about how bad it was in the city for the people—and for Mother's sister, Queen Kaylan. She'd heard them saying that the queen had given Mother something to hide. Whatever was going on had them very concerned and they wanted to do something to help. And now they had been gone so long.

Right before they left, Mother had taken Brinid to her room and given her a very strange piece of material, ripped on one edge, and unlike anything she'd ever seen before. She'd taken it out of a small basket and showed it to Brinid, calling it a parchment map and insisting in her strongest, this-is-extremely-important voice that Brinid must take care of it no matter what. Not really understanding at all, Brinid had nodded in agreement since Mother's voice made it sound so important. Ever since they'd been gone, Brinid had kept it with her in her knapsack. The first night when Mother and Father had not come back, she had sat down in the corner, carrying the knapsack with her and stuffing it behind her back.

But they'd been gone so long. And she was so hungry. Light had come and gone twice. This time when it was dark again, she was more scared than before. And more hungry. She now clutched her knapsack like a pillow, afraid to leave her corner in the dark.

* * * * * * *

The Genesis of Atron

At last the light began to chase away the shadows where Brinid had fallen over onto the floor and slept. As the sun hit her eyes, she awoke quickly, deciding that she was so hungry she would have to venture out to find something to eat. She stood and stretched, leaving her knapsack on the floor. Maybe the neighbor would help her. She and Mother talked often and borrowed things from each other.

Walking next door, Brinid knocked softly, hoping someone was home. When no one answered, she knocked again a little more loudly. Finally, the neighbor's husband opened the door just a crack. Seeing Brinid, so small and scared, he called his wife. She brought Brinid inside and made her a morning meal with some cheese, bread and dried meat. Brinid sat quietly eating at their table, not saying anything, afraid to talk. At last she felt full again, but did not know what to do next. The neighbors tried to tell her what had happened the last few days.

"Little One, the days have been bad," the neighbor lady began. "The Unidans made a Raid here in the city and tried to take away the king's crown. They had help from some people here in Tolden. It was a very dangerous thing to try and their plan didn't work. Now they are all dead."

The neighbor paused and looked at her husband before continuing. "We are certain your parents were among those working with the Unidans, and they are dead." She laid her hand on Brinid's arm.

Brinid stared straight ahead without moving, beginning to cry softly. She felt numb with pain; all alone and hopeless. She put her head down on her arms and buried her face, sobbing louder. *How could this be?* she thought. *What will happen to me? What do I do now?*

The neighbors waited.

2009 Barbara Moon

The Genesis of Atron

Finally Brinid lifted her head, her green eyes overflowing with tears. She looked around the room, down at her empty plate and then back at the neighbors with a sad question in her eyes.

The wife spoke for them all, slyly cutting her eyes at her husband. "You can stay with us, Dear. We'll help you." Her husband nodded.

"Come. I'll go with you to your house and help you bring things over that we can use. Your parents won't be coming back."

Brinid could hardly bear hearing that she would never see her parents again. She barely understood that everything had changed. Her mind began to race. *What about the castle . . . and Aunt Kaylan? What about Eric? What happened to them?*

It was too much for such a little one. *But I can't go to the castle,* she realized. *It would not be safe if Mother and Father did what she said. I have no one. No one. I'm all alone.*

Like a person sleepwalking, Brinid stood up and went towards the door. She quietly opened the door and walked towards her home. *I have to get the parchment,* was all she could think about. *I have to get the parchment. Mother said I have to take care of the parchment.*

The neighbors followed.

While the neighbors were taking whatever they could find of value back to their house, Brinid was in her room stuffing the parchment to the bottom of her knapsack and covering it with some clothes, her cloak and a few belongings precious to a little girl of six seasons. For lack of knowing where else to go or what to do, for now she would go back with the neighbors. But already she was sensing deep inside that she could not trust them. She would watch everyone around her carefully-- and most of all she would guard the parchment-- because Mother and Father said she must.

CHAPTER FIVE

It had been a whole season since Brinid had moved in with the neighbors. During that season, Brinid had grown quieter and quieter, seldom interacting with anyone. Her little heart was guarded against anyone who might possibly hurt her. Immediately after moving in with the neighbors, she had watched them strip her parents' house of everything. They fed her and gave her a place to stay, but there was no real kindness offered, no loving touches or helpful words. Her biggest fear was that they would discover the parchment that she always kept hidden from others' eyes. She'd almost forgotten what had happened a season ago, blocking most of it from her mind, but in spite of that, deep feelings she could not put into words drove her to protect the parchment at all costs.

Unable to bear the lonliness and fear of discovery any longer, Brinid now had a plan. She'd been hiding food in her room for a while, taking things that would not spoil quickly, and soon she was going to run away. Quite often she'd thought about going to the forest and living by herself. Tonight the thoughts were stronger, *I won't be any lonelier in the forest; no one cares anyway, and nobody can find the parchment there.* The more she thought about it, the more she wanted to do it. Finally she made her decision. "I'm going!" she determined aloud.

Collecting the few items she could call her own and putting them into her pack on top of the parchment, Brinid prepared to follow through with her plan. *I have some food and my cloak. I'll be alright,* she reassured herself. *I'm going tonight. I doubt they'll even look for me. Besides, I can take care of myself.*

The sun was setting, darkening the streets. Brinid lay awake waiting for everyone to go to sleep. Soon the house was quiet, the streets mostly deserted. Grabbing her knapsack and putting on her cloak, pulling the hood over her braided hair and around her face, she stole out into the night. Slipping alongside the buildings, she made her way to one of the gates. Waiting patiently, she watched until she saw the guard turn the corner towards the next gate. As soon as he was out of sight, Brinid ran off into the woods.

* * * * * *

Brinid was not enjoying her time in the forest like she'd expected to. It had not taken very long for her to run out of food, she had no way to make fire and all through the nights she heard too many unknown rustlings in the dark. She'd found a little creek not too far into the forest, staying there beside it for days. She was afraid most of the time, but the parchment brought a sense of comfort whenever she drew it from her pack and held it. There had been no rain and no people to bother her, but hunger and fear were once again driving her decisions. She was going to have to go back to the city.

As Brinid slipped past the guards and back into the city, nobody noticed another child walking alone in the streets of Tolden. It was common. Sometimes the children banded together and other times they went about alone. Brinid preferred to be alone. It was easier to get the food she needed if she were by herself. When the shop keepers were busy with a customer, she could grab whatever she had her eye on and run quickly away. Sometimes they shouted after her, but seldom did anyone catch her.

As time passed, Brinid grew wiser in the ways of living on the streets, learning to take things from someone's robe or pocket without them knowing it. When she found coins dropped on the ground, she bought something to eat instead of stealing it. When all else failed, she scrounged through the trash in the alleys for something to eat. All the love she'd felt and all the lessons she'd learned from her mother and father were lost as she continually stole and lied in order to live.

As another season passed, eventually a day came when Brinid no longer knew who she was or where she had come from. Occasionally when she had chosen, or been forced, to live with one of the Tolden families, unspeakable things had happened. Brinid pushed those memories from her mind until they too no longer existed. Each time she escaped from a terrible situation, she had more determination than ever to take care of herself, vowing anew to never trust another person. If she passed the castle, a place she used to visit with her mother, it meant nothing more to her than a place where someone might throw out some scraps that she could rummage through and find a bite to eat.

Living on the streets became a way of life that was almost bearable in its familiarity and routine, safer than being with others, until one day as Brinid reached out to grab a piece of fruit from a stand, the unthinkable happened—a large hairy hand clamped down on top of hers, encircling both her hand and the piece of fruit.

"Caught you in the act!" a gruff voice growled above her head. Dropping the fruit, Brinid looked up into the face of one of the king's guards, a large, heavily bearded man with ugly scars on his face and mean looking eyes. She tried to pull away, biting his hand, twisting her body and kicking at the guard's shins.

"You're not going anywhere except with me," he said, jerking her arm and picking her up around the waist. "You're going to the fields with the rest of the scum. You can work there for a while and see how you like that, you little thief. The Unidans will keep you company and the king will have another worker to carry water and bring in his crops." Frantically clutching her pack as tightly as she could in her free hand, all Brinid could do was kick the air as he carried her off.

CHAPTER SIX

Working in the fields was very hard work. Since the drought had worsened, it took many hours of backbreaking trips to the big river to carry hide buckets to the ditches that helped irrigate the fields. The older workers labored daily to extend the ditches to connect the water to the fields, but until they were finished the younger workers had to carry water when ordered to, leaving their hoeing and weeding for another day. Brinid believed that it gave the guards great pleasure to watch them work. She had observed them secretly sabotaging the ditch digging in order to keep its lengthening at a minimum.

Life wasn't much better at night when the workers finally dragged themselves back to their rough tents to eat and rest. They barely had the strength to make a fire and cook a meal. Brinid stayed away from the others, especially the Unidans, not knowing exactly why she singled them out in her mind--it was just something there. The Unidans were always talking softly to each other and trying to help the other prisoners when they could--or when they were allowed. Brinid wasn't the only one to shun them, even though they often smiled at the others around them. She noticed their kindness to other Toldens, but it had little effect on her toughened heart. They were always telling stories, speaking of a better life, possible even in the midst of hardships and trials. These stories only angered Brinid. She grew to hate the Unidans and refused to sit around their fire pits and listen to their stupid talk. *Trust no one,* her mind raged. *No one! Find a way to escape. Protect the parchment.* These were the thoughts that occupied

The Genesis of Atron

Brinid's every waking moment. She carried her pack on her back while working and slept with her body curled around it at night.

Part of another season passed slowly. The nights were growing cooler and Brinid had to use her cloak for warmth. At last one evening the guards seemed less alert than usual. Brinid, always observant and cautious, thought perhaps the time had come that she might be able to get away. When the rest of the workers bedded down for the night, Brinid remained awake, only pretending to sleep, her head near the opening of the tent she shared with some other young ones.

The crescent moon rose, covered mostly with clouds. The guards slumped at their posts snoring loudly. Brinid raised her head slightly and looked around at the sleeping camp. Very quietly and slowly she rose to her knees and began to crawl out of the tent. Just as she did a few years earlier after leaving the neighbors' house, she hugged the sides of the tents, moving cautiously. She reached the crude fence and wiggled under it. *I'm free again,* she shouted inside her head, picking up her pace on hands and knees until she could finally stand up and run, the precious knapsack flopping on her back. *I'm finally free again! I have to answer to no one.*

Not having many options for finding food sent Brinid back to the city. Settling back into her routine of living on the streets alone brought Brinid little true satisfaction other than the freedom she had to do as she pleased. She still felt the pangs of hunger nearly every day. But doing as she pleased, trusting no one, and answering to no person felt good in the moment. Brinid did not realize that what she thought of as freedom was really a lie. Each time she separated herself from the possibility of connecting with others, her heart grew harder inside.

On the outside, though her cloak and boots were tattered and worn, Brinid appeared healthy and strong. But the appearance of strength was also a lie. Deep down inside, the little girl that used to belong to

Darrias and Jired was there, hidden and covered with pain. As hard as she worked each day to stay alive on the streets, she fought even harder at night to keep the little girl buried deep inside. Most times, she could make herself believe that being alone and trusting no one was best.

But some nights, huddled almost invisibly in a corner on some Tolden city street, Brinid would hear a whispered question flicker through her mind. As she wrapped her cloak tightly around herself before sleep overtook her, it would come: "Will I ever feel happy and safe--will I ever have a home and someone who cares about me?"

Made in the USA
Columbia, SC
18 February 2025